Moore, Katharine
M~~~~~~~~~ house

DATE DUE

OCT 2~	
NOV	
D~	
D~	
FEB 6 1987	
FEB 2~	

Moore, Katharine
Moving house

14.95

DATE	ISSUED TO
OCT 2 0 1986	
NOV 1 1986	
DEC 2 - 1986	
DEC 1 2 1986	
JAN 7 1987	
FEB 6 1987	

DISCARDED

MOVING HOUSE

Also by Katharine Moore
and published by Allison and Busby:

Fiction:
Summer at the Haven
The Lotus House

For children:
The Little Stolen Sweep
Moog

Non-fiction:
Victorian Wives
She For God: Aspects of Women and Christianity

MOVING HOUSE

a novel by

KATHARINE MOORE

ALLISON & BUSBY
London · New York

First published in 1986 by
Allison and Busby Limited,
6a Noel Street, London W1V 3RB
and distributed in the USA by
Schocken Books Inc.,
62 Cooper Square, New York, NY 1003

Copyright © 1986 by Katharine Moore

British Library Cataloguing in Publication Data

Moore, Katharine
Moving house.
I. Title
823'.914[F]   PR6063.061

ISBN 0-85031-671-5

Set in 11/14 Palatino
by AKM Associates (UK) Ltd, Southall, Greater London
Printed and bound in Great Britain
by Billings and Sons, Worcester.

To Anne Dickenson

Chapter 1

Clare Curling was writing a letter, sitting in her suburban garden in the spring sunshine. Her three children, wholly ignoring each other, were playing round her. Patrick, the eldest, aged eight, was systematically beheading the daffodils; Becky, aged five, was whirling aimlessly round and round the lawn; Bertram, aged three, clad according to his latest whim in a cast-off pink muslin dress of his sister's, was laboriously pushing a large toy car up and down in a straight line, up and down, "over hill, over dale", like a bulldozer.

Clare, looking up and seeing the destruction of the daffodils, called out, "Stop that, Patrick! The poor flowers!"

"They're enemy outposts — there's a war on, I can't reduce the invading force."

Clare sighed and folded up her letter. "It's lunchtime," she said. "It's so warm, we'll have it outside, come and help carry the dishes out."

The two elder children came.

"And how have you been amusing yourself this morning, Mother?" enquired Patrick kindly.

"I've been writing to Granny. Bertram, come to lunch."

"No," said Bertram. It was the first time he had spoken to anyone that morning, but he could have been heard

1

chanting to himself resolutely: "Two, twenty, three, ten."

"He's got to push his car one hundred times to and fro," explained Becky.

"But he doesn't know how to count up to a hundred," said Clare.

"No," agreed Becky, "he might go on for ever; we shall have to push food into his mouth as he goes along."

"You could stop him, Mother," suggested Patrick, but Clare only sighed again. She did not feel like a confrontation with Bertram that morning.

"You spoil that child," said Patrick, but the subject did not interest him. "Which do you like best," he continued, "Norsemen or Vikings? I like Vikings."

"Aren't they the same?" said Clare.

"I hate Romans best," said Becky, "I hate Romans much the best, don't you, Mummy?"

Her mother made no comment — she was thinking about Bertram. She didn't believe she spoiled him, she just couldn't do anything about him. That dress, for instance; he'd tripped over it twice already and got a nasty lump on his forehead. Besides, she didn't fancy having a transvestite in the family.

"What children have you got, Mrs Curling?"

"Oh, a boy, a girl and a transvestite."

Bertram was like his grandmother, she thought; you simply couldn't influence either of them once they had made up their minds, and they were both always making up their minds.

"Are we going to stay with Granny soon?" asked Patrick. "Will she let me wind up the grandfather clock, do you think? She said I could next time we came, but she might not remember."

"No, we can't go just yet," said Clare, "she's had a fall and hurt her leg."

"Well, I fell out of the pear tree and hurt mine, but I

2

could see people while it was getting better."

"But she's old."

"Oh, very, very old," said Becky. "She'll die soon, won't she?"

"You shouldn't say things like that," said Patrick, who was fond of his grandmother when he had time to think of her. "There's lots of people older than Granny who aren't dead."

Becky nodded, "There's Mr Jackson — he's very old; he hasn't any teeth."

"He's only a toad in a book, silly," said Patrick. "Toads aren't people."

"I hate toads best," said Becky dreamily. "May I have Bertram's tomato, please? I've eaten mine."

But just then Bertram came up, silently climbed on to his chair and began to eat his peas one by one with his fingers. Clare pushed a spoon at him, but he disregarded it. It was surprising how quickly the peas disappeared.

Yes, thought Clare again, *he's just like Granny — contra-suggestive. And now it looks as though she's going to be a problem — she really ought not to go on living at that place on her own, but I doubt very much if she'll hear reason.*

Roberta Curling, the incipient problem, was in reality the children's great-grandmother, but this fact was all but forgotten. She had made an early marriage, and her only child had done the same. Her son and his wife had died tragically in a road accident, leaving twin babies to be brought up by their young grandparents who had, in every sense but the literal one, been Mother and Father to them. When Patrick was born, Roberta had refused to be labelled a "great" and as she was both firm and active no one thought of her as such.

On this particular day she was also writing a letter, propped up in bed and fighting against the drowsiness

3

induced by her pain-killer. "You will soon be hearing from Clare," she wrote to her granddaughter in Austria, "perhaps you have already done so. This is just to say — don't be worried, I am quite all right. I had a little fall and have damaged my knee, entirely my own fault, slipped on the basement stairs, too much in a hurry as usual, you will say, and you will be right, but it's hard to change the habits of a lifetime. Anyway, no bones broken, and Nurse Higgins and dear Mrs B. are taking good care of me. Clare is certain to fuss, so don't take any notice. She and Alex will be on at me more than ever to leave Rowanbank, but I don't mean to. The question is, will you back me up? I am not sure of this."

She lay back on her pillow, tired. No, she was not sure of Naomi. Alex she could fathom easily, but Naomi. . . . She thought of her with love, longing and irritation. Roberta shut her eyes and there she was before her, one of the many Naomis — this time a dryad disguised as a schoolgirl, absorbed and grave, and in her grandmother's eyes utterly charming, playing her flute under the walnut tree. Naomi was musically so talented, and after her school-days were over the way to a promising career had seemed to be opening out. But she had gone off to Salzburg, inspired by a suggestion of a fellow music student. And she had fallen in love with Salzburg. "There's a river," she wrote home, "a perfectly useless river running through the very middle of the town — you can lie on its banks under flowering chestnut trees — and, in a park, another river of white tulips, miles long, that winds away among the grass and the towers, all different shapes and colours and the mountains in a circle all round."

That was all very well; but next she fell in love with a young Austrian doctor, with a taste for music, though very much dedicated to his work, and they were married. Early and rather precipitate marriages did run in the family, Roberta grimly admitted. Then Naomi, without a struggle

4

and apparently with complete content, had dwindled into nothing more than a wife. It was two years ago now since all this had happened and there were not yet even any children as an excuse for giving up her career. She still played, of course, but never professionally and she had only come back to England twice since her marriage and then with Franz, who couldn't take much in the way of holidays, and Naomi would not leave him.

Still, thought Roberta resolutely, *I must not repine. She is happy and she might have died that time when she was so ill as a baby.*

A knock came at the door, it was Mrs Baxter from the cottage; it was always known simply as "the cottage" because it was the only one near and it had had Baxters in it ever since Roberta had known it. The current Mrs Baxter sailed into the room like a duchess. She had immense but comfortable dignity. She "did" for Roberta and obliged extra in emergencies.

"I'll boil you an egg for your tea and I'll leave you a thermos of coffee so you won't do so badly till Nurse comes," she said, "for I am that sorry I can't stay this afternoon, as William's not so well."

"Oh, dear," said Roberta, "you shouldn't have had to leave him. I'm sorry to be such a nuisance."

"Don't fret," said Mrs Baxter. "I'll be back before he comes in, only I wanted to be there and have his supper ready and the fire bright for him."

"I'll soon be about again," said Roberta. "I mean to hobble round the room tomorrow."

"You must be careful, though," said Mrs Baxter, "it's falls that lie in wait for many when they're getting on, and stairs especially. You ought to have asked me to fetch up those apples. I don't hold with you going down into the cellar, if you don't mind my saying so."

Roberta, when left alone again, lay looking out of her window, watching the late pale spring sunshine filter

5

through the interlaced branches of the walnut tree. She was wondering if she herself ought to hold with going down into her cellar any longer. It was stupid to have continued to keep the store of apples there, but there they had always been kept and she had never thought about any other place for them. When you had lived a long while in the same house, it was difficult to adapt even in details to the exigences of age.

She reluctantly allowed that Alex and Clare might have some reason on their side, for it was true that the house was not really suitable for her any more, in fact had ceased to be so years ago — an inconvenient rambling, servant-planned building, not even very attractive to look at, with far too big a garden but an incomparable view. Here, in the middle of a field, long ago, her mother had sat herself down and said to her father: "This is where you must build me a house." He had gone straight off to bargain with the farmer who owned the field, leaving her sitting there in entranced contemplation, and in no time the house was built. *You could do those sort of things then*, thought Roberta. *How spoilt they were, those Edwardian middle classes, until their sons were taken away from them to be slaughtered.* Perhaps after all her parents had been glad then that she was Roberta and not Robert; for she was a disappointment: they would have preferred a son and there were no more children.

The home was named "Rowanbank" because its site was bordered by an old hedge containing a rowan tree greatly prized by her mother — "A magic tree," her mother had told Roberta, "full of power to keep evil away." It had been of reasonable size at first and used only as a country retreat from Highgate but, as the years passed, a study library was added here, an extra bedroom there, in preparation for her father's retirement.

Rowanbank became Roberta's at his death and, as things turned out, she continued to live there after her marriage.

Charles did not mind where he lived as long as he could paint, bless him, and there was plenty of room for that and for her mother to live with them. Here her son was born, here she had brought up his children and there was plenty of space for them too. She had never thought about the appearance or convenience of the house, it was simply home to her. The view miraculously had remained unspoiled. Beyond the garden, so lovingly planned by her father, whose hobby it was, stretched Kent hop gardens and cherry orchards, flanked by gently sloping wooded hills, then a stretch of marsh and on clear days the blue line of the sea. No buildings were anywhere to be seen, except a cluster of hop kilns, their white cowls cocked up into the sky like some curious land-locked sailing craft. One of Roberta's bedroom windows looked out on this view, the other on to the walnut tree.

But it was too dark now to see out of either and her knee had started to ache quite badly. Willow, her large grey tom cat, who adored people in bed, had come in through the door left ajar by Mrs Baxter and, carefully searching out the injured leg, had settled himself heavily upon it. She was very glad to hear Nurse Higgins's car.

Having let herself in and come up the stairs, Nurse Higgins asked: "Well, and how are we feeling this evening?"

Roberta wondered why double vision so often afflicted Nurse Higgins, but she accepted this odd fact without irritation, for her touch was gentle and she brought with her the benefaction of cleanliness and order.

The next day Roberta felt distinctly better and more able to cope with life, which that morning contained Clare's letter, a succession of anxious chirps: "Do hope you are better, so unfortunate, knees are very tricky, wish so much I could come and look after you, but it is Patrick and Becky's holidays still and they are at home all day and, even if I could find someone to look after them, I should have to bring Bertram with me, I am afraid, as he is going through a difficult stage just at present, am so glad that you have dear Mrs B. and that you find Nurse Higgins so helpful and the neighbours too. That is the best of living in a village, though of course Rowanbank is not really in the village and Alex and I both wish you were not so isolated except for Mrs B., in fact we do wish you were nearer to us. It would be so nice if we could have you living here with us at No. 30."

May you be forgiven, Clare, you think no such thing, poor dear; and heaven knows I don't either. Roberta paused in her reading of the letter at this point and lost herself in memories of Alex and Clare's house. The recollection made her draw her bed-jacket close round her. Neither of them felt the cold, letting windows and doors stay perpetually open for the convenience of the children and Boffin the cat. She had long had a closed season from November to March for her visits there, but the English climate was no security for warmth at any time. Then the one small spare room had no space for clothes (the wardrobe and chest of drawers being filled with the family's overflow) except for one peg and, with luck, one little drawer. As for the children, she was very fond of their company in small doses, but they seemed omnipresent from early in the morning, when both Becky and Bertram loved to invade her narrow bed, till late at night; like most children nowadays, they kept the same hours as their elders. There was a show of getting Bertram off earlier, but he never failed to reappear in his night garments to be greeted with resigned indulgence. There was no children's room, so their games, toys and garments were everywhere. Roberta liked order and the haphazard ways of the household harassed her. Meals were at odd and arbitrary hours and very healthy, vegetarianism being one of the many "isms" Alex loved. He would soon have trouble

8

with Patrick about that one though, thought Roberta, remembering an occasion when the boy had enquired suddenly: "Why is it wrong for me to eat meat but all right for Boffin to eat mice?"

Alex's job was in town planning but he also served assiduously on many local committees — UNA, CND, gipsy welfare and Friends of the Earth — in all of which he was supported by his wife. Both of them were ardent idealists; however, whereas Alex devoted himself to his causes with something of the same pleasurable ardour as his grandfather had for his painting, Clare's commitment was strained. She typed endless letters, arranged coffee mornings and put up in the little spare room various visitors, from respectable or near-respectable lecturers to down-and-outs.

The trouble was, thought Roberta, that she had been brought up from childhood to be too unselfish. This, unless you had a strong natural zest for life, was apt to get back on you. Clare had too low a level of personal enjoyment. Even with her family, although she undoubtedly loved Alex and the children deeply, she somehow seemed not to delight in them — or not often.

Roberta turned again to the letter:

But as our house is really too small to make you comfortable, Alex and I do hope, dear Granny, that you will think seriously whether you shouldn't leave Rowanbank, for since this fall we are anxious about this. You know Alex is on the committee of a very well run Home for the Elderly at Penge. You would be within easy reach of us there and Alex wants to know if at least you will let him put your name on the waiting list. It is so popular that there is quite a long list always.

Yours affectionately, Clare.

P.S. Patrick is writing to you — it is his own idea and he

will not agree to enclosing it in mine, so I do not quite know when you will get it as he is always busy about something or other.

Roberta slowly pushed the letter back into its envelope. What a fuss about a silly little fall! *No, no, my dears, not for me your Home, however popular; I shall stay on at Rowanbank until they carry me out in my coffin.* But her irritation was tempered by a little pleasant warmth, aroused by the postscript. She was touched by the fact that Patrick had thought of writing to her, even if he never actually finished or posted it. He was her favourite of the children. She *liked* him as well as loved him. He already showed signs of possessing more practical ability and common sense than anyone else in that family, and these were qualities that she valued.

When Patrick's letter did arrive some days later it did not disappoint her. It said:

Dear Granny,

I am sorry you have hurt your leg. Is your grandfather clock keeping good time? I think I shall learn how to make clocks when I am older — they are most interesting. At present I have invented a loom. I am making mats on it. I have made a green and red one and a blue and yellow, the fasteners off of them is not very good yet. When I get it right I will send you one and I think I will inclose a plan with instrucsions for making a loom like mine and if I were you I would try it yourself.

Yours faithfully, Patrick.

Roberta smiled and looked carefully at the plan for the primitive loom. She thought it neat and ingenious. *Perhaps he really has a turn for invention — much more useful than the arts these days. I suppose, considering his background, that he had to begin with looms, but it'll soon be computers and robots, I expect.*

She was downstairs again and getting about with two sticks, though the knee was still painful.

"I'm afraid it won't be all that reliable in future," said Dr Thompson. "Knees are tiresome. Still, you won't want to be seeing me any more for the present. I'll get the physiotherapist to look in and give you some exercises and Nurse will help you for a bit longer. But watch out on your stairs — it's a long way up to your bedroom, isn't it? Do you ever think you'd do better now in a flat or a bungalow?"

"No," said Roberta, "I hate flats and bungalows and don't intend to have another fall."

"Well, well," said Dr Thompson, assuming his best soothing manner, "I'm sure you'll be careful, though it gets less easy to avoid trouble with advancing years, Mrs Curling."

That makes three Jeremiahs, Roberta reflected to herself after he had gone, *four, if you count Alex and Clare as two. I wonder who will be the next.*

The next was her cousin Kitty who came down from London for the day to see her.

"Every time I come here the place looks larger and shabbier," Kitty said cheerfully over lunch. "All the carpets are wearing out; you'll trip over them next and they'll cost a fortune to replace — there's yards and yards of them. And as for the garden! Doesn't William Baxter work for you any longer?"

"He's been under the weather with his arthritis for quite a while now, poor fellow. It's as much as he can do to get through his work on the farm; but he'll do what he can for me once he's better. It's been such a wet spring. Yes — perhaps things are wearing out — what else would you expect?. . . But how can the house look larger?"

"Well, it does, I can't think why you stay on here, Berta — it would give me the creeps. Aren't you afraid at nights?"

"Why on earth should I be? What is there to be afraid of?

11

Rowanbank isn't haunted, it's not old enough."

"I'm not thinking of ghosts, silly — don't you ever read the papers or listen to the news? Old ladies living alone are beaten up or murdered every night."

"No, I don't read the papers or listen to the news if I can help it, at least not that sort of news, though if I did I bet they'd tell me that far more people are killed on the roads than murdered in their homes, yet it doesn't keep you out of your car."

"But I'm forced to take that risk or I'd never go anywhere. You're not forced to stay on here alone in this barracks of a place. Well, you always did know your own mind and I won't go on about it . . . I only meant to help. . . . Let's talk about something else — your view is as lovely as ever anyway."

Roberta, who had been thinking how tiresome Kitty could be, melted at once; besides, she felt she had had the best of the argument and she was really very fond of her cousin.

After Kitty had gone the phone rang. It was Naomi.

"Is anything wrong?" enquired her grandmother anxiously — it was not yet time for her usual monthly call.

"No, I'm fine, but I've had your letter and Clare's and really, dear, though I know she fusses, I do agree with her this time. Besides, it isn't only her, it's Alex too. Do think about it, don't just refuse because they're urging it."

So, clearly Naomi was *not* going to back her. The very idea of moving from Rowanbank! She might have considered it if the place was really like an old barracks, as Kitty had called it, and therefore bare; but it was more like a furniture depository stuffed from top to toe with the accumulation of years, and everything encrusted with memories and associations.

She looked at her husband's big oil paintings that covered the walls. They were workmanlike, very well painted, but old-fashioned in subject and treatment, faith-fully representational; colour photography had really made them superfluous, she thought sadly. Still she loved them, not only because she, at any rate, thought them beautiful, but also because they reminded her of holidays they had spent together. Besides the landscapes that dominated the dining- and sitting-rooms, there were stacks of canvases in his studio — then there were all the books and her parents' solid large Victorian and Edwardian furniture and the few antiques that she and Charles had collected. . . .

Oh, no, it was hopeless, she and Mrs B. together could manage quite well, she felt sure, in spite of all this uncalled-for advice and admonition. Deciding not to bother any more, she went to sleep.

The real and decisive blow came some weeks later. Mrs B. was very late arriving — an unheard-of event — and, equally strange, she actually hurried as she came up the path to the kitchen door. As soon as she got in she sat down heavily on the nearest chair and began to weep. Roberta, who propped on one stick had been slowly stacking up the breakfast things at the sink, was struck with horrified amazement. There is something quite appalling in witnessing the breakdown of what has hitherto seemed an unassailable and blessed bulwark against misfortune.

"Oh, whatever is the matter?" she cried.

Mrs Baxter spoke between sobs: "It's my William, he's fell off a ladder almost as soon as he got to work. They came to tell me from the farm. His bad leg must've given way — it has been worse lately. They've brought him home."

"But," said Roberta stupidly, "you mustn't stay here then, you must go to him."

Mrs Baxter looked up at her, "Do you think I'd be here if he'd wanted me any more?" She was in command of herself now that the news was out and it was Roberta who was crying.

"You mustn't take on," she said. "It was God's will."

Roberta stifled a quick dissent; what was an outrage to her she saw was Mrs Baxter's one comfort.

The funeral was a week later. William Baxter had been widely loved and respected in the village and the new grave in the old churchyard was heaped with the bright flowers of spring.

"Grandpa's flowerbed is better than yours," said Mrs Baxter's youngest grandson, who had come with her to see Roberta the following day.

"You go and play with Willow, dearie," said Mrs Baxter. "You can give him his dinner if you're careful — it's all ready on the kitchen table. He asked me what a grave was," she explained when he had disappeared. "Someone had told him his grandpa was down in the grave now. I don't want him to think like that, I said it was grandpa's flowerbed and we'd come back and plant a rose tree on it later and now he's going round saying his grandpa's flowerbed's the best in the village."

The little boy's mother was Mrs Baxter's only daughter; she had two sons besides, one farming in Canada, the other in the navy. She was going to live with this daughter who kept a guest-house at Ramsgate and she had come to tell Roberta this.

"The cottage is tied, but you'll know that. Mr Chittenden wouldn't turn me out right now, don't think that, but I know he needs it and I can be of use to Betty: her husband's not up to much, though she won't admit it, and there's another baby on the way. I'm glad to go really, only I'm that worried about leaving you here all on your own, how will you manage?"

How indeed! thought Roberta. Then something seemed to snap in her brain and she heard herself saying: "You won't have to worry, Mrs B., for I'm going to make a move too — but that's between ourselves just for the present."

Mrs Baxter's face cleared. "Oh, well, I *am* glad; fancy that now, it seems meant, doesn't it? No, no, of course I won't mention it to a soul and I'll not be going myself yet awhile. There's a deal to see to first, so I'll be coming along as usual for the time being. I dare say it'll be as long as you want me."

Chapter 2

The decision seemed very sudden set off by Mrs Baxter's tragic news but Roberta realized that the skies had been gradually darkening since Kitty's visit. For instance, she had begun to notice things — stains and cracks, pieces of rotten woodwork, some patches of damp and a general air of dinginess. *You don't see wrinkles and lines on a loved familiar face until someone from outside remarks on them*, she thought, *and then you seem to see nothing else.*

She was now able to hobble round the garden. There, spring with its terrifying splendid growth had been this year left a free hand. Strong unpruned shrubs were thrusting aside the rarer timid plants, and the weeds! — not the pretty feathery wild flowers: cow parsley, campion, clover, sorrels and moon daisies that had in early summer once grown in the field before it became a garden, but huge fierce nettles, and thistles and docks in the corners; thick carpets of ground elder seemed to flourish everywhere while festoons of ivy spread across the paths and smothered the two lovely stone urns her father had brought from Greece long ages ago. Even the lilacs and the snowball trees had grown too large and straggly and failed to comfort her. She bent down in feeble protest to tug at some couch-grass rooting in the lily bed but found she couldn't straighten up again and would have fallen had she not clung to her stick. *Old age, really, why need it be so spiteful!* She had returned to the house a little shaken.

Now, after Mrs Baxter had gone, Roberta sat in the kitchen for a long while apparently doing nothing. Actually she was busy enough at the always unpleasant occupation of facing facts. Could the Baxters be replaced? Only by a miracle. There used to be no such problems, but now it seemed less and less possible to get anyone to do anything. No doubt she could be allowed a home help and "Meals on Wheels", but though that might keep her afloat it couldn't save Rowanbank. Could she or ought she to live on here with the place decaying all around her? Dry rot, wet rot, she saw them like little demons grimacing at her out of the shadows cast by the jungle outside that, growing and thrusting up and up, finally quite blocked out her view, while she herself, a cross between Miss Havisham and the old Queen in the Sleeping Beauty's Palace, dreamed and mumbled, covered with cobwebs, in a corner.

"No! If I can no longer cope with Rowanbank it must go to those who can," she said at last, and roused herself to finish the washing up.

But where could she go? Not to Alex's irreproachable Home, that was certain; nevertheless it would be nice to have some alternative before she let her family know that she was now prepared to leave. Barring the Home, probably everyone would expect her to find some convenient corner in the village. Actually she knew of three cottages that were or soon would be vacant, but to live so close to Rowanbank and not actually in it was somehow unthinkable. Besides, the cottages were too familiar. How could she ever feel that poor Alice Rose's little sitting-room, where she had often drunk tea from the best china that was kept in the alcove to the right of the fireplace with the portrait of Alice's mother over it, belonged to her? Could

17

she presume to occupy John and Rachel Turner's marital bedroom after they had moved away to Folkestone, or invade Mrs Vincent's kitchen? It was impossible.

The more Roberta thought about it the more she felt that if she could not go on living at Rowanbank (and it seemed clear to her now that she couldn't) it would be better to make a clean break. It came to her in a flash that she would go back to Highgate, the only other place in the world where she had roots: had she not been born there and run about its streets as a child? It might do better than anywhere else to end there also.

She decided to consult Kitty. Kitty was the nearest to a sister that Roberta had known. She was six years younger, a gap wide when very young but narrowing with adolescence and negligible in middle age. Now, however, it was observable again, for Kitty was still mobile and energetic, running a shop and a library service for her local hospital and dashing about everywhere in her mini. She had lived in London all her life and had a flat in Islington.

"I'm glad you've seen sense at last," she barked briskly down the phone, "though very sorry about William, and I must say I think it very good sense, Berta, to come back to town. It'll be much easier to find the sort of thing you want — you're not going to be silly about flats, I hope?"

"Now don't bully me," said Roberta.

"As if I could, but if I did it's only what you deserve, my dear. Heavens! How you and Rollo used to boss me about in the old days; and you bossed Alex too, that's why he's so keen on the underdog now."

"Look here," said Roberta, "I'm not paying for this sort of talk, even if it is at the cheap rate. What I want to know is, will you find me somewhere to go as soon as possible? And I don't want Alex and Clare to know till I've burnt my boats."

"I'll do my best. It oughtn't to be too difficult. As soon as

18

I've anything in view you'd better come up and stay for a night or two."

"Thank you," said Roberta. "I'd be very glad to do that."

Kitty's flat was much more comfortable than Alex's house, and Roberta always enjoyed her visits there. The curious thing was that Kitty herself seemed incapable of benefiting by its comforts. She had an odd way of kneeling on the floor instead of relaxing into one of her charmingly easy chairs. A favourite occupation was to play intricate games of Patience, kneeling there, talking volubly all the time, with the cards spread out before her on the carpet. She seldom bothered to take off her coat or change her shoes once she had put them on in the morning and this gave her an air of impermanence.

"You call in at your flat," said Roberta, "you don't live in it. And why don't you get a decent television? Everyone looks terribly ill on this one, and they all have green hair."

Kitty, kneeling in front of it, simply giggled. Roberta wondered why she found this endearing, while if Clare had so behaved it would have irritated her. *It's because I love Kitty, I suppose, and accept the whole of her, whereas I'm just fond of Clare and don't accept much of her at all.*

Not very long after she had consulted her, Roberta found herself at Kitty's in order to view a flat which she thought might do for her.

"If you should take to it, it would save a lot of trouble in the future and it really would be lucky to have found somewhere so soon."

It was one of a small complex planned for the elderly but not the incapable. Each flat had a fair sized sitting-room, a small bedroom and a still smaller kitchen and bathroom. The flats were perfectly private and independent of each other and there was a nice neutral warden who was only called upon in emergencies. The situation was quiet, facing a small, slightly dingy square garden for the common use of all the tenants.

"It's not a bad outlook from the front," said Kitty, "but the bedroom looks out on to a blank wall — do you think you could stand that after your view?"

"There was plenty of sky," said Roberta, "and do you know, I believe a blank wall might be better than ugliness."

"The kitchen's dreadfully small."

"I liked the kitchen; its fittings are so ingenious, like a ship's cabin, you couldn't be untidy in it, there wouldn't be room."

"So you really think you'll put in for it?" said Kitty.

The flat they had seen was still occupied but was to become available in the near future. Roberta optimistically hoped that she would have sold Rowanbank by then or at least that the dates would show a reasonable co-operation.

"Yes," she said decisively, "I want something settled in my mind and I don't see that I could do much better than this. I'd only be wasting your time; and I can't keep on coming up to town to look at places."

"What will you do about Willow?" asked Kitty. Sadly, but understandably, pets were not permitted at Coleridge Court.

"Willow wouldn't transplant to town life anyway," said Roberta. "I'll have to find a home for him in the village." She would miss him but he had not proved one of her favourite cats. His mother had been both more intelligent and more affectionate. She considered Willow greedy — unless she were in bed he preferred the kitchen and Mrs Baxter to her company, but she could recommend him as an excellent mouser and he was undeniably handsome.

"Well, don't blame me if you don't like it when you get there," said Kitty. Whenever she succeeded in influencing her cousin she experienced a sort of fearful joy. Twelve years old had once declaimed to six years old: "I'm twice your age and therefore twice as clever." "You're not, you're not!" shouted affronted six years old, but secretly feared that twelve years old was right.

"Of course I shan't," said Roberta, "I'm truly grateful to you, Kitty."

As a matter of fact the whole business had taken on an air of unreality and it was as if in a dream that she asked the Warden to put down her name for No. 14 Coleridge Court and paid a deposit. This mood persisted when she wrote to tell Alex of her plans. It seemed as though she was inventing a passage of some imaginary autobiography. She enjoyed it. She decided to imply that it was largely owing to Alex and Clare's advice that she had made up her mind to leave Rowanbank, thus softening her absolute refusal to consider their wonderful Home for the Elderly. *And even if they don't swallow that*, she thought, *it's a gesture.*

"Well!" exclaimed Alex on reading her letter. "It seems that Granny has decided on quitting at last."

"Really!" said Clare.

"She says she has come round to our way of thinking: I shouldn't wonder though if William Baxter's death hadn't something to do with it."

"Why, isn't Mrs Baxter staying on at the cottage?"

"She doesn't say."

"Is she going to take up a place at Fairlea?"

"No, she says she wants to go back to the Highgate district. Kitty's already found her a flat somewhere. Apparently it's all fixed up."

"I think she might have consulted you first," said Clare.

"Oh, I don't mind as long as she gets Rowanbank off her back. She wants me to run down and see her to talk it all over as soon as I can spare the time."

"And when will *that* be?" said Clare, frowning. "Your diary's absolutely full up for ages."

21

"I shall have to fit it in somehow," said Alex cheerfully. "I must say I'm relieved, I thought we'd have a regular tussle to move her and that she'd leave it too late. I'm sorry she's not going to Fairlea, though. She'll be no nearer us at Highgate than she is now."

"Oh, so am I," agreed Clare emphatically, and she really did feel sorry because it was not going to happen. She even caught herself indulging in a sense of grievance because Roberta was turning to Kitty for help instead of to her. *Why do I want what I don't really want?* she asked herself anxiously.

It was only during Alex's visit that the reality and magnitude of her decision began seriously to dawn upon Roberta. She was about to break up her home, to destroy what was a living rich entity with which she had an immensely strong personal relationship and to replace it with an alien little box that had nothing whatever to do with her. Was this madness or was it sense? But William Baxter was dead, Mrs Baxter was leaving the village, Rowanbank was falling to bits, "change and decay in all around I see". It was not she who was committing this outrage, it was Time.

Alex had put the house into agents' hands and was now suggesting an auction of its contents — "There's a lot of furniture to be got rid of and the books — some of those must be quite valuable. I think an auction is really necessary, Gran."

"Yes," said Roberta mournfully, "but you and Clare and Naomi will want some things, I hope. I should like Patrick to have the grandfather clock."

"That's good of you," said Alex. "Now don't worry about anything — I'll see to all the business side of things. I know it's a wrench for you but I'm absolutely sure you're doing the right thing."

But after he had departed Roberta looked round

22

about her and despair once more seized her.

"I must make a list," she said to herself, "that will help me, several lists in fact." She had always been addicted to making lists. Almost as soon as Roberta could write, her nurse used to find, stuffed into secret corners of the nursery, lists of her toys (the dolls with their names and ages), lists of her pets, and later on she made lists of her teachers and schoolfellows, carefully graded as "very nice", "nice", "harmless" and "horrible". She continued through life to make lists, of books that she had read during the year, of those she meant to read, lists of Christmas and birthday cards; even making out shopping lists gave her a sort of satisfaction. She supposed she liked lists because they imposed order, which she liked, on confusion, which she feared. But now, faced with a more chaotic state of affairs than she had ever known or, she hoped, would ever have to face again, she found herself disinclined after all to begin on any of the required lists. Instead she thought she would write to Patrick about the clock. *No, I will phone him,* she decided, *I'd like to hear his response.*

Alex had not yet thought to mention the matter. He was enjoying a rare time of leisure with his family in the garden. It was a lovely day and everyone including Bertram was in a genial mood. Clare was sewing, Patrick reading, Becky drawing houses with beautiful bright red roofs and Bertram was again busy with his car, now filled with as many of Becky's dolls as could be squeezed into it. Then, suddenly deciding that he would prefer it to carry bricks, he called out:

"Becky, will I bring your children back to you, shall I?"

"Yes," said Becky.

It took him some time, since he was at the bottom of the garden and the car had to be carried up some steps, but he arrived panting and pleased and unloaded the dolls.

"They cried all the way up," he remarked complacently.

"What for did they cry?" asked Becky.

"Well, I doesn't like them and they doesn't like me," said Bertram.

"What for don't they like you?"

"Cos I think they've got silly-looking faces and *so* I doesn't like them and *so* they doesn't like me."

"But they likes me," said Becky.

"Oh, yes, they likes you," said Bertram.

"Why do they like her?" enquired Alex, who had been following the conversation with interest.

"Because *she* doesn't mind them having silly-looking faces," said Bertram, "and so they likes her."

"Yes, they likes me," said Becky, disregarding, however, the heap of dolls at her feet and adding another lovely red house to her drawing.

"I wonder if Bertram is going to be a philosopher," said his father, and Clare immediately had a vision of her younger son lecturing in a university hall to a crowd of enthusiastic students. Was it Oxford or Cambridge? She knew that ideologically she ought to have preferred one of the modern universities, but there were certainly towers about and the Hall was panelled. She was drawn back to the present by the telephone.

"I'll go," she said, "and then I'll see about tea."

But she came back almost at once. "It's Granny," she said, "she wants to speak to Patrick. Whatever for, I wonder?"

They soon knew. Patrick came flying out of the house shouting: "She's going to give me the grandfather clock, Granny's giving it to me for myself!"

"Good gracious," said Clare, "she can't."

"Why do you say she can't, Mother?" said Patrick. "She can, can't she, Dad? I think it's super of her."

"Oh," said Alex. "She did mention it to me, now I come to think of it. What's the problem?"

24

"Where on earth can we put it? There simply isn't room," said Clare.

"Sorry, dear," said Alex, "I never thought of that, but I'm sure we'll manage somewhere."

"We might build a tower for it in the garden," suggested Patrick, "or we could make a hole in the dining-room ceiling so that it could poke through into mine and Bertram's bedroom, then you'd never feel lonely when I wasn't there, Bertram, because it would go on talking to you. I shall never forget to wind it up and so it will never stop talking."

"All through the night?" asked Bertram in sepulchral tones.

"Yes, all through the night. You'll like that, won't you?" said Patrick.

"No," said Bertram.

Clare agreed with him. She remembered that the clock, a handsome very large mahogany Victorian piece, had a particularly penetrating chime. Really, Alex might have had more sense; but then men hadn't, even the nicest of them. Now it was impossible for her to refuse to have the clock without mortally offending both Patrick and Roberta. The only place for it, she thought in despair, would be in the hall round the corner by the stairs, but that was also the only place to keep the family's coats and shoes and where a most useful row of pegs and a basin would need to be removed.

"I want a clock," remarked Becky, "I want a clock much the best."

Bequests are sometimes tricky, even more so perhaps when the donors are still alive. Roberta had not meant to embarrass Clare, she had thought only of pleasing Patrick and of keeping the clock in the family. It hadn't even looked particularly large to her in the lofty hall of Rowanbank. Similarly, though far from unimaginative, she failed to

25

envisage the suitability of Charles's paintings in different surroundings.

Dr Thompson had always particularly admired a menacingly dark mountain storm scene that hung above the wide fireplace in the dining-room.

"I'd so like you to have that," said Roberta when he came to give her a final check up. She wasn't to know of the conversation that would take place when Dr Thompson took it home.

"I couldn't say 'no'," he told his wife, "she meant it so kindly and it is a good painting; after all it might be worth quite a lot one day. You never know with pictures."

"You'll have to hang it in the surgery," said his wife grimly, looking round her pretty pastel-coloured sitting-room, "and I only hope it doesn't frighten the patients as much as it does me."

Then Alex, who so seldom wanted anything for himself, expressed a strong feeling about a needlework stool, a golden gentle Venetian lion on a crimson background which he asserted he had loved from babyhood. But Kitty laid claim to it, as it had been worked by her mother. In the end, there was feeling on both sides which was unpleasant, though Alex gave in.

Naomi was simply vague. "You know what I'd like, Mother," she said, but Roberta didn't know, nor what she would be prepared to pay to take back with her to Austria.

Value, sentiment and utility were all complicating factors in the division of goods, which Roberta had supposed a simple matter. And she still had not begun on what Alex said should be her first concern, those articles she herself was going to take with her to Coleridge Court. The problem of Willow, the cat, also worried her. She had not yet found a home for him. All animal-lovers seemed already to possess a cat or a dog or both, and Willow, she knew, would never take to sharing; he was a born individualist.

It was a thoroughly disagreeable time but Roberta supposed she would get through it somehow — the sense of unreality was still with her and was a help. Mercifully too Mrs Baxter was as good as her word and, stoutly refusing to leave the cottage until Rowanbank itself was vacated, came in to do for Roberta as usual. Since William's death there had been a growing bond between the two women. Roberta had begun to call her Ellen, a familiarity she had never presumed on before, and it seemed welcome. She looked forward to seeing her and to discussing their mutual problems.

One morning Mrs Baxter put down a saucer of milk for Willow, who sniffed at it as if it were poison and then walked away.

"He'll come back to it," said Mrs Baxter. "Have you placed him yet, Mrs Curling?"

"No," said Roberta, "and I *don't* want to have to take him to the vet."

"Well, now," said Mrs Baxter, "I was wondering, Betty's old Dinah has had to be put down; she had bronchitis, poor thing. I could ask if she'd mind me bringing Willow with me. It won't be what he's used to but the children are good with animals and there's a fair piece of garden."

"Oh, Ellen! That would be a relief," said Roberta. "I'm sure he'd be happy with you — he's always preferred you really."

Willow had returned to the milk, finished it, washed up and polished the plate and was now regarding them with a fixed intensity.

"He knows we're talking about him," said Mrs Baxter fondly. But it was really only a flea, which when located he dealt with proficiently.

"I wish I could do something for *you*, Ellen," said Roberta. "I suppose there's none of my things you'd fancy?"

Mrs Baxter shook her head. "I'll take the will for the

27

deed, dear," she said. "I'll only have the one room and that I'm sharing with Lenny after the baby comes, so there'll be very little I can take."

"Oh, dear," said Roberta, "what are you doing with all your things then?"

"Will's brother's coming for them with his van — my niece, she's getting married and setting up a home and 'll be glad of them so I haven't near so much bother as you have."

"But don't you mind parting with everything?" said Roberta.

Mrs Baxter stopped what she was doing to consider.

"I don't know that I hold much with minding," she said at last in her calm, curiously impressive way. "There's always something to be going on with. No, I'm not troubled. I've arranged with the vicar about keeping Will's grave nice; I'm sending something regular — not that I think of him as there of course, only he always liked to have things neat. It worried him lately about your garden."

"Yes, I know," said Roberta. "I'm sorry."

That day, after Mrs Baxter had left she sat for some time thinking. At length, "There's always something to be going on with," she quoted to herself. She took a sheet of paper from her writing desk, sat down and headed it:

List of articles to be taken with me to Coleridge Court.

She paused and looked round the room. Opposite her she saw a branch of the walnut tree and the portraits of her father and mother hanging above her bed. But it was not the actual tree nor the real portraits that she was looking at, rather their reflections.

No. 1, she wrote, *The Mirror*.

Chapter 3

" 'How nice it would be'," read Roberta's mother from the Alice book, " 'if we could only get through into Looking-Glass Land! I am sure it's got such beautiful things in it.... Why, the glass is turning into a sort of mist now, I declare. It'll be easy enough to get through,' and certainly the glass was beginning to melt away just like a bright silvery mist."

Roberta sat up straight on her mother's lap. "Is it true?" she asked.

"Of course, it's true," said her mother, "magic is always true." And then Nurse came for her to put her to bed and her mother closed the book.

"Oh, can't you go on and Nurse go away?" said Roberta.

"No, darling, you'll have to wait till tomorrow evening but I'll tell you now if you like that Alice *did* get through into Looking-Glass Land."

The next day when she was left alone and no one was in her mother's room where the mirror hung — the big oval mirror that Roberta admired so much — she stole in quietly. The mirror had two little gold boys on top of it, holding a crown of gold leaves between them. On the dressing-table below were two cut-glass scent bottles with silver stoppers and a silver-backed hairbrush and comb, and a beautiful little china tray on which a shepherd in a blue coat was bending over a shepherdess in pink, and looking as if he were just going to kiss her. Roberta loved this tray but now she had eyes only for the mirror. She pushed a chair up close to the dining table and climbed upon it, just as Alice had climbed on to the chimney piece, and she looked and looked and it did seem to her as if the room in the mirror must have something wonderful and exciting round the corner that you couldn't see. She began to press against the glass, feeling it all over, but it did not melt for her as it had done for Alice. She pressed and pressed; being an impatient child she began to get cross. Then it struck her that magic didn't always work the same way in stories; but if her mother said it was always true, it was only a question of finding the right way to go about it. Perhaps this looking-glass had to have a door made in it. She looked round for a tool and decided the back of the hairbrush would do. She lifted it up and with both hands hit the mirror a resounding crack. She was a strong child for her five years and there was a splinter of broken glass while the brush, rebounding from contact with the wooden back, flew out of her hands, fell on the china tray and broke it in two. Roberta, standing on the chair among splinters of china and glass, began to cry with disappointment and sorrow. There was no looking glass land after all and the beautiful tray was broken so that the poor shepherd and shepherdess were parted for ever.

But now the room became full of cross surprised scolding people, and rage was added to despair.

"What a wicked little girl!" said Nurse.

Roberta, climbing down from the chair, tried to hit her and burst into a passion of sobbing.

"Stop now, Roberta," said her father. "You've done enough to upset Mama already." He bore her away and his authoritative but calm tone of voice and his large pocket handkerchief reduced her sobs gradually to silence.

"Now tell me," said her father, "what made you go

30

smashing up all Mama's pretty things of a sudden?"

"I was only trying to get through into Looking-Glass Land like Alice. Mama said it was magic and magic was always true but it wasn't true," hiccupped Roberta.

"Now listen," said her father, "magic is true always for Mama, but for you and for me, Roberta, it is different, do you understand?"

She nodded. She did not understand, of course, but dimly she saw that there was something to be understood. She was also for the first time aware that, though a divinity to be worshipped still, Mama was not always to be depended on.

"But the poor shepherd and shepherdess," she cried.

"Who?" said her father. "Oh, Mama's tray — I expect that can be mended and the mirror too; if not, we must buy her another mirror and another tray."

"But they won't be the same," said Roberta.

And though the mirror had a new glass, which looked too bright and clear for its frame, and the tray was stuck together cleverly so that you could only see a tiny line dividing the two little figures, things were actually never quite the same again.

By the time Roberta had reached her tenth birthday she was tall enough to see over her mother's shoulders the reflection of her face as she sat before the mirror. Her father was clasping round her neck a new necklace. It was of greenish-blue turquoises to match her eyes. They were lovely eyes with dark curling lashes and finely arched eyebrows and the face was a classical oval like a Botticelli goddess. It was pale like a Botticelli too with a flowerlike clear pallor that added to its charm. Her father also was looking at the reflection and smiling.

"Why does Father always give you a present on my birthday?" asked Roberta of the face in the mirror.

"She's jealous," laughed her mother.

31

"Well, I give you one too," said her father. "Didn't you like it? I thought you wanted a watch."

"Oh, yes, of course," said Roberta, "I didn't mean that."

But they neither of them answered her.

Long ago, naturally, she had asked her mother the usual questions of how she had come to have a birthday at all.

Her mother's eyes shone perilously. "Well," she began, "well, darling, have I never told you? It was like this; one day I woke up early and I heard a great whirring and a beating of wings at the window. I jumped out of bed and looked and I couldn't see the sky at all for the rose-coloured feathers of a huge bird with eyes like emeralds and a golden beak outside my window. He swooped past once, twice, but the third time he perched upon the sill and I saw that on his back, nestling among those glorious feathers, was a tiny baby girl who stretched out her arms to me — and that was you!"

"Was it?" shouted Roberta. "And what did you do?"

"Of course, I leaned out of the window and caught you up and the bird flew off at once and vanished high up above the clouds."

This story had charmed Roberta until she grew too old to believe it, or possibly she had never really believed it, not at any rate after she had broken the mirror; and later, instead of pleasing her, it began to haunt her. *Perhaps I am adopted,* she thought, *perhaps this was just Mother's way of telling me I'm not really their child at all.*

At last, making her voice sound as matter-of-fact as possible, she said one day to her father: "By the way, I've been reading a story about a boy who was found as a baby and adopted. I'm not adopted by any chance, am I?"

Her father laughed. "My dear Roberta, come and look in Mama's mirror. Now don't you see, you and I have got just the same sort of eyes — cat's eyes my mother called them, a queer kind of yellowish colour that polite people call hazel;

32

and I'm afraid you've got my big nose too and jutting-out chin. It's hard luck on you, my dear, to have taken after me so obviously but you've got your mother's hair." He pulled Roberta's thick fair pigtail. "Well, now are you satisfied?"

By that tenth birthday, however, she knew that babies came out of their mothers but she did not know how they got there. Children were never then taught the facts of life, they just picked them up or didn't, as the case might be.

"Does it hurt getting the babies out?" she asked Rose, her best friend, who was a mine of information.

"Yes," said Rose, "and sometimes you die."

"But why don't men have babies?"

"I don't know, they just don't, and it's their fault too. I don't quite know how yet, but I don't think it's fair."

Roberta thought this conversation over. Perhaps it had something to do with the presents to her mother on her own birthday. Later, once when she was spending the day with Kitty, her aunt came in from a neighbour's and exclaimed to her uncle: "Thank goodness Bessie's baby's come at last. It's a boy. I'm afraid she's had a bad time but it's all right now."

"Oh, what's he like? Did you see him?" asked Kitty, but Roberta said:

"Did Mother have a bad time when I was born, Aunt Margaret?"

Her aunt looked flustered. "Oh, girls, I didn't notice you. Whatever makes you ask that, Roberta?"

"I just wondered."

"Then you needn't wonder any more. You mustn't think all babies are difficult. You behaved very well I remember and gave your mother little trouble. Of course," she added, "your father made a fuss, perhaps you've heard something, but he makes a fuss if she pricks her little finger."

Roberta said nothing. She was aware, and not for the first time, of an edge in her aunt's voice when she spoke of her mother. It was not at all what she was used to, for everyone else seemed to adore her. Her mixture of beauty, gaiety and a sort of innocent silliness combined with that indefinable grace, which is called charm, was generally irresistible. Men of all ages were her slaves and her husband accepted this with pride, for he was confident in her absolute reliance on himself. As for love, there are infinite varieties of this. When she was old enough to observe such things, Roberta sometimes thought there was little difference between her mother's love for her father and her own, and that her relationship with other men was rather like a little girl's pretending to be grown up, pleased with admiration, expanding like a flower in its warmth but never in the least troubled.

The years passed, but her mother's face in the mirror hardly altered. Roberta, now in her mid-teens, was watching her sitting in front of it trying on hats. Beside her, thrust anyhow into an old blue and white pitcher, was a bouquet of flowers: pink roses, pale blue delphiniums and purple columbine. There was never anyone who took less trouble than her mother arranging flowers, Roberta thought, yet the effect was often unpredictably perfect.

"I look a fright, a perfect hag."

"Of course you don't, Mother."

"Yes, I do, none of these hats will do. Ever since I sold that little black one to my dear, dear friend Helen, I have wanted it desperately. I really must get it back from her."

"Why on earth did you sell it then?"

"I suppose I must have wanted the money terribly for something and your father must have been away. I thought I had too many hats but I was completely mistaken. Now what am I to do?"

"Why can't you wear that lovely one with the curling feather that makes you look like a Gainsborough?"

"Too big, especially in a storm."

"But it's perfectly fine."

"Not when I wear that hat, it always turns to thunder then — there must be something sinister about it. No, I shan't wear a hat at all, just a wrap, I think." She threw a rose-coloured scarf round her head. To Roberta it was as if the little shepherdess on the china tray had stepped out of her Virginian landscape into Looking-Glass Land. She said so.

"Darling, you are sweet," said her mother, "but where is my shepherd? Immured in London, poor fellow. Never mind, I'm going to meet my knight instead."

"Old Sir Joseph?" enquired Roberta. Sir Joseph Maxwell was the squire of the village and owned the woods around Rowanbank.

Her mother nodded. "Do you know, Roberta, I was walking in the woods one day and I sat down to rest under our special oak tree — the one you used to love to climb — and Sir Joseph came riding by on his great horse and he dismounted and bowed to me and said: 'Lady of the woods, you must not sit upon the ground. I shall have a seat put here for your own particular use.' Yesterday he sent the word that it was there ready for me and I am to meet him there this morning."

"Is this true?" asked Roberta. She never knew.

"True, true, true, as true as Una and the Red Cross Knight in the dark forest," her mother said, and left.

"It's a lovely seat," she told Roberta and her father that evening, "and actually inscribed with my name. Do, do both of you come now and see."

"I've got my preparation to do," said Roberta.

They were spending most of the year at Rowanbank by now and she had wanted to go with Rose to one of the new big public schools for girls, but her father had said: "We want our only child at home," so she attended classes in Hastings instead. She knew that if she had been a Robert, though still an only child, there would have been no question of staying at home.

" 'O fret not after knowledge, I have none

And yet the evening listens.' . . . Remember Keats's thrush, Roberta," said her mother.

"But I'm not a thrush," said Roberta and would not go. Birds, for her mother, she reflected, were never themselves, always voices or spirits.

The years ticked away on the grandfather clock. Roberta was now so tall that if she wanted to look into the mirror she had to stoop or sit on her mother's chair, for she had inherited her father's height as well as his looks. Her mother seemed a sprite beside her. *So much change in me,* thought Roberta (she was nearly twenty-one), *and so little in her.* For there was not a grey hair in her mother's head, nor a wrinkle in her face. But her father, on the other hand, seemed suddenly to have aged and to be always tired. He had become very thin and his skin, instead of being tanned by the summer's warmth, was dry and sallow. He had been away for a few days, ostensibly on a visit to his brother's home, but Roberta anxiously suspected it was to consult their old family doctor in London. Her mother had noticed nothing wrong — or had she just shut her eyes to it? One could not tell. She did not seem at all troubled the evening he was expected back.

"Read me some poetry, Berta," she said.

"What shall I read?" asked Roberta obediently.

"Tennyson, I think. Yes, I feel like some Tennyson today, anything that comes."

Roberta took down the volume and it opened at "The Lady of Shalott".

" 'And moving through the mirror clear

That hangs before her all the year,

Shadows of the world appear —' " She had got thus far when she heard her father's step on the stairs.

36

"Hallo, my dears," he said. "Reading poetry?"

He bent over Roberta and took the book from her; turning the leaves, he read out the last verse himself:

"'Who is this and what is here?
And in the lighted Palace near
Died the sounds of royal cheer.
But Lancelot paused a little space.
He said: "She has a lovely face.
God in his mercy grant her grace,
The Lady of Shalott."'"

His voice broke and Roberta looked up quickly.

"You look very tired, Father," she said, "let me get you something to eat." She got up but he followed her out of the room.

"You mustn't worry your mother by saying things like that in front of her," he said. "I'm all right, only a bit washed out by the journey in this heat. I don't want any food. I think I'll go and have a swim, that always makes me feel better. Don't wait dinner for me — goodbye."

He sounded brusque and, a little hurt, something made her go to the door and wave him off. He waved back and that was the last she saw of him.

They found his clothes in his usual favourite bathing spot, folded up carefully — he was always neat — but they never found him, and Roberta was sure that that was what he would have wished. "He was such a good swimmer," they said, "it must have been a sudden attack of cramp."

The next day the letter came for her. Her father knew that she was always down first in the morning and collected the post. As soon as she saw the writing she took it up to her room. It was very short and said: "I have inoperable cancer. Your mother must not be subjected to the strain and ugliness that my probably drawn-out illness would cause her. This is the last thing I can do for her, for she will be able to bear it much better this way. You will

37

keep my secret and there is no need to ask you to cherish her. You are my good daughter. I have left all my affairs in order. God bless you."

She sat with the letter in her lap for some time and then she found some matches and burnt it and went down to breakfast.

Her mother, thought Roberta, was one of the few people who could cry without making herself look hideous, in fact her tears seemed only to add to her appeal, making her eyes look larger and more vivid in colour. She had wept quietly all the previous day but she was not crying any more now.

She looked up as Roberta came in and said, "It was such a beautiful way for your father to go, wasn't it, darling, at sunset, with the sea like a shimmering pearl? I noticed it especially that evening."

"Yes," replied Roberta, but to herself she was saying: *How can I bear this romanticizing? You can't romanticize death, it is too big. A beautiful way to go — to go where? To some island of Avalon I suppose. "A woman incapable of tragedy"*, where had she heard that and about whom? Then she rebuked herself for this bitterness. Tennyson's poem still rang in her ears. Was not her mother another Lady of Shalott, sheltered behind the magic web of her father's protective love that had kept her away from reality, among "her space of flowers", in Looking-Glass Land to the end?

It was too late now for any change and, as far as Roberta could tell, the spell was never broken, for after her father's death, her mother withdrew further and further away into her dream world. She managed even to evade the reality of her own ageing and death. She never went grey, instead her hair became a moonlit instead of a golden halo round the smooth face and her eyes, lovely still, gradually grew vacant, the enchanting smile meaningless.

The grandfather clock struck the hour, but in what year?

At first Roberta simply could not think and was it in her mother's room or her own that the mirror, which had ceased to reflect anything at all, was now just a dim oval shape in the darkness? Slowly the present imposed itself once more upon her consciousness and she pulled her ageing bones out of her chair and switched on the light.

Chapter 4

Roberta decided that, what with the mirror and book-shelves and cupboards, there would not be room for many pictures on the walls of the little flat at Coleridge Court. The bedroom was really very small; she would keep her family photographs there and she must make her choice of only three or four paintings for the sitting-room. It was a difficult and distasteful problem, for Rowanbank was full of pictures, most of them Charles's, and she must decide which of these to keep, which were really her favourites among them. Only the smaller ones would be practical, she feared; the others, if they could not be disposed of among family and friends, she supposed must go into the auction. But there was one other picture that she must certainly keep besides her husband's — it had belonged to Rollo, her cousin, Kitty's brother and her first love. To part with this would hurt — yes, even after all these years.

Rollo was only two years older than Roberta and this is no barrier to a companionship if tastes are shared so, whereas Kitty was held to be too young for her brother's pursuits, Roberta, who was what her elders disapprovingly called a tom-boy, was his inseparable ally.

"I don't like your friend Dick," she had said to him when they were children.

"Why?" asked Rollo. "He's a nice boy."

"No, he isn't; he thinks I'm no good because I'm a girl, but you don't, do you? Because you know I'm really a boy."

Whatever Rollo did, Roberta had to do too. "They egg each other on," was the general complaint. Neither had any sense of physical fear, but Roberta, being the younger, often came off the worst in their scrapes. Rollo's passion was for climbing roofs, trees, rocks, the higher and more perilous the better. Both children seemed to have charmed lives, but several times Roberta fell and each time bore her bumps and bruises with nonchalance so as not to call down vengeance on Rollo, who had whispered: "Good for you, Bobs" — recompense enough. He was a nice-looking boy, with very blue wide-open eyes and freckles, about which he was sometimes teased.

"Well, I like them," declared Roberta, "and Mother says they show you are favoured by Apollo the sun-god, you know."

"She *would*," said Rollo but added, being no less under his aunt's spell than the rest of mankind: "She can if she likes, but I won't have anyone else talking such rot about me."

When tired of more active pursuits, he and Roberta would devise adventure stories and then act them out, with Kitty dragged in to be a squaw or a cabin-boy or a prisoner.

Childhood passed, the long days grew shorter and soon began to race past. Roberta, now in her teens, still knew and thought nothing of sex. She liked being with Rollo better than with anyone else, but she took him for granted. In that Freud-free world she remained utterly ignorant and unconcerned, though when she did give any such matter a thought it seemed as though it was rather fatally easy to find yourself having a baby. The Bible, an irreproachable if not very explicit source of information, spoke simply of "knowing each other", whatever that might mean, and in Shakespeare's *A Midsummer Night's Dream*, which they did one term at school, Hermia seemed mysteriously anxious for Lysander to "lie further off". Then there was *Adam Bede*: Hetty and Arthur just met each other in that summerhouse and it seemed that neither of them thought anything special had happened; it was weeks later before poor Hetty knew about the baby.

Roberta had been reading the book one holiday when Rollo and Kitty were staying at Rowanbank; she was fifteen by then. She and Rollo had been for a long bicycle ride together and had flung themselves down on the sweet-smelling Downland by a dew pond to rest. They were lying so close together that she felt the warmth of his body and saw the little beads of perspiration on his forehead, and that night she lay awake worrying. She had certainly "lain with him" and she didn't want a baby at all. It would ruin her chances of being captain of hockey. Besides, she did at least know that it was considered terrible to have a baby without being married, *Adam Bede* had taught her that. Well, she couldn't help it — if it happened, it must. But it didn't, so that was all right. But as far as excitement went, Miss Godfrey, her darling games mistress, was a far greater source of thrills than Rollo.

The following year she was sent to a convent school in Bruges to improve her French and to learn not to be such a hoyden, and then she was brought home again in a hurry because of the War. What with all this, she and Rollo saw little of each other until she was seventeen and he had just left his public school. Then he came for another visit and things were changed; they were still good companions, but he looked at her in a different way and this made her look at herself differently too.

"I like that yellow dress you've got on," he said one day.

"It matches your eyes. I don't know anyone else with little gold flecks in their eyes like yours, Bobs."

"Father has, he calls them cat's eyes," she said quickly, because she felt suddenly shy though pleased. Fancy Rollo making her feel shy!

But the last evening of his stay she took care to put on the yellow dress again and something made her pin a yellow rose at her neck. After dinner they were left alone, her parents having gone for an evening stroll. Rollo chose a record, a collection of songs, and put it on the gramophone — a new acquisition with a huge blue and gold horn. The songs were mostly old and sentimental, the last was her mother's favourite "Roaming in the gloaming with my sweetheart by my side".

"Well, let us go roaming, shall we, Bobs?" said Rollo when it was finished. "We may as well follow the example of our elders, but we'll take a different path, I think; they went to the woods so we'll go through the fields."

They went into the garden full of the evening scents of white jasmine and late-flowering honeysuckle and the heavy scent of elder flowers shining like multitudinous small moons in the dusk. As soon as they had gone through the gate with the meadow beyond, Rollo put his arm around her, turned her face to his and kissed her gently. It was the first kiss she had ever had that meant something special and, though it was so gentle, the memory of it was to remain with her — a part of her life always. But he soon took his arm away and began to talk eagerly.

"I'm going to join up of course now I'm eighteen. I shall join the RFC, I've quite decided on that and I can't help hoping the war won't be over before I've had a go. You'd like me to be in the RFC, wouldn't you — rather than the other services, I mean?"

"Oh, yes," said Roberta, thrilling to his enthusiasm, even though she could not help a little stab of fear.

43

"After the war I'll go to Oxford; the parents are set on that. But I mean when I've finished there to take up engineering, I think, because I really want to build bridges and railways and things in Africa or somewhere the other side of the world. You won't mind that, Bobs, will you? You'll marry me, won't you, and come with me?"

"Of course," assented Roberta. It seemed both beautiful and inevitable and her heart danced with joy, in spite of that small creeping shadow; the war couldn't go on much longer anyway.

He was off early the next day.

"Rollo and I are engaged," she announced to her parents after he had gone.

"How sweet, darling," said her mother.

But her father said: "You are much too young, both of you."

Rollo adored his training. He wrote Roberta letters that were full of the exhilaration of this new element he was exploring. "Every time I go up, there is this terrific feeling of power when the plane takes off, spurning the old earth, and in a few moments there I am higher than the highest mountains — amazing!"

There were his companions too — all marvellous, according to him, but especially his Squadron Leader — "not what you'd expect somehow, an amazing sort of chap, paints in his spare time and reads poetry. He's lost an arm and that's why he's training us now. He sells some of his pictures, sometimes in aid of the Red Cross. I've bought one, I'll bring it home on my next leave which, with any luck, will be my last before I'm off on active service."

But Roberta didn't see the painting until a good deal later on. It was spring when they heard that he had been shot down but had managed to make a forced landing behind the front line and was in hospital with a broken leg. Roberta was arranging daffodils in a bowl when her father told her the news, and suddenly she felt fully conscious of the fear that she had all this while refused to contemplate. "Now," she said to herself, "now there is a future."

The end of the war was at last in sight and, because of his leg, Rollo's demobilization came through quickly and he was able to enter his father's old college. Just before Armistice Day, Roberta was allowed to go up to Oxford with her aunt and Kitty to help settle him in. She always afterwards saw the city in her imagination as it was then — the trees golden against the grey stone walls, the misty faint luminous river, dahlias still smouldering in the college garden round which Rollo proudly limped as if he owned it all. He was simmering with high spirits. It was as though the horrors that had engulfed so many of his generation had passed him by and the whole of that visit seemed to Roberta to be blissfully and simply happy. A sort of unacknowledged capitulation had apparently taken place among their elders. She knew that they still considered her too young for a proper engagement and also that both sets of parents disapproved of first cousins marrying, but she and Rollo had no reservations. Rollo bought her a string of amber beads at a little shop in Ship Street and when he gave it to her they both became very serious.

"I'm saving up for a ring. I want you to have something really nice; you shall have it by Christmas," said Rollo.

His rooms in college were, so his mother pronounced, both dark and poky, but Rollo was delighted with them. The painting he had written about had pride of place above the mantelshelf. It was an arresting picture that looked as if it had been hurled on to the canvas: it was nearly all of the sky, great clouds, thick and solid; below, darkness with the suggestion of roofs and chimneys, and then, in one corner, a break in the clouds and a bright patch, flying into the midst of which was a tiny plane.

"When I bought it, do you know what he said to me,

45

Bobs?" said Rollo: " 'I'm glad you're the one getting that picture, young Connolly, but look here, that plane's not a bomber, you can see that, can't you? It's a civilian plane.' Yes, he said that as if it were important."

"It's so small, I don't see how anyone could tell," said Roberta.

"Oh, I can tell all right and I can see the pilot too; bomber or no bomber, I bet he's happy."

"I wonder if I shall ever fly," said Roberta.

"Of *course* you will, everyone will be doing it soon. We'll fly together to wherever I'm going to build my bridges."

The letter she had after that visit was as buoyant as ever. Men were coming up now from the services and he had met an old RFC pal who greatly admired his picture, work was fine, everything was terrific, but people had begun to go down with that beastly Spanish flu germ that was going round everywhere, a fellow he coached with, a terrifically good chap, had it, he hoped it wouldn't reach Rowanbank. "Always your Rollo." There was a postscript about Armistice Day: "Glorious, wish you had been here, we painted the Caesars' heads red — the ones outside the Sheldonian, you know, fine old bastards, they look as if they enjoyed it; brightens them up no end. Will tell you more next time."

But there was no next time. Aunt Nell was summoned to Oxford after Rollo had been found slumped over his books in the grip of the terrible post-war influenza.

"It is mostly the strongest who get it worst," said the doctor. "They won't give in until it is too late."

Rollo's temperature soared and after a few days' struggle his heart gave out. There was nothing to fight the germs with but aspirin. Whole colleges became hospitals, and the bells were tolling as if the great Plague had come to Oxford again.

"He never knew he was dying," her aunt told Roberta. "I'm so thankful for that, he loved life so, even in his delirium he seemed happy — he talked continually of flying and he spoke often of you. 'Bobs, Bobs,' he kept on saying, 'I must tell Bobs.' I want you to have that picture he was so fond of, I am sure he would wish you to have it."

Roberta, as she now looked at Rollo's picture, wondering where she would hang it at Coleridge Court, saw it again with attention for the first time for many years, while thoughts of Rollo came flooding back. With his death, something had also died in her. *Bits of us are always getting killed and other bits are born*, she thought. With Rollo had vanished her age of innocence — there was to be no more "piping down the valleys wild"; the joys that came later were no less, perhaps even greater, but they were certainly different. She wondered, not indeed for the first time, what her life would have been like had Rollo lived. It would probably have taken her away, far away from Rowanbank, it would at least outwardly have been more eventful and exciting and they would have been happy together, she was sure, as they had always been. But to what depth this happiness would have reached she was not certain. Their young love had grown between them as naturally as if it had been born with them — it had been like spring water rather than wine.

She decided she would hang Rollo's picture above the door in the new flat and the bookshelves would go against the wall facing the gas fire, free for at least two of her husband's paintings. Which should she choose?

Chapter 5

There were so many of Charles's pictures, he had been a prolific painter and during the latter part of his life his pictures had gone out of fashion and he had not sold many, so there they were on the walls of Rowanbank and stacked in his studio. He had never been, as he would ruefully agree, a very original or inspired artist.

"Well, I think it's lovely!" Roberta would say.

"No," said Charles firmly, "it's lost the spark — of course it was there to begin with or I never would have started, but it's got lost on the way. Never mind, I can always have another go."

Roberta was completely sincere in her admiration, for she never asked that a painting should do anything but faithfully recall a scene or an object that she thought beautiful and this her husband's pictures invariably did. She was not therefore, she was ashamed to admit, now concerned with which were Charles's *best* pictures but merely with what they represented. She also had to consider their size. Her first choice was a watercolour, subdued in tone, of a cluster of grey roofs in the foreground and, beyond, a wide stretch of moorland.

Charles Curling had literally jumped into Roberta's life. It

48

was nearly a year after her father's death, her aunt had packed her mother and herself off for a holiday in Scotland. They were to stay at Dunfermline with Kitty's old governess, Miss Jamieson, known as Jimes to all the family. Jimes now kept a small very select guest-house in that historic town and Aunt Nell had the satisfaction of killing two birds with one stone.

"You both need a holiday and Jimes needs guests now that the holiday season is over. You can have a few days in Edinburgh on the way, everyone should visit Edinburgh once at least."

They had both loved Edinburgh — Roberta for its architecture and grand views and her mother for its romantic associations: St Margaret and Robert Bruce and Mary Queen of Scots and Bonnie Prince Charlie, all mixed up together in her glancing butterfly mind. Roberta would have liked to have stayed longer but Jimes was expecting them and was not one to be kept waiting, so they caught the prescribed train. Just as it was leaving, the door of the carriage was flung open and a strange-looking young man flung himself and his bag into the corner opposite Roberta, who was first alarmed and then annoyed. *He might have hurt himself and perhaps he means no good*, she thought, for it was not a corridor train and she had always been warned to look out if a man invaded a carriage containing only one or two unprotected females. At first his looks did nothing to reassure her: he had a scar running down one cheek, his eyebrows were non-existent and, although he was young, his hair was quite white. He was no albino, however, for a pair of very alert grey eyes met hers and then crinkled at the corners as he smiled and apologized. She felt at once that there was no cause for alarm but she was still annoyed, especially as he began at once to make conversation. Roberta did not approve of people who talked to strangers in trains.

49

The young man had noticed the guide book on Roberta's lap. "This your first visit?" he enquired and then, as they drew free of the station, he began to point out places of interest.

"See that imposing building? Queen Victoria took a fancy to it. She asked the city to give it to her but they refused so she never came here again. It's a hospital now."

"Really," said Roberta, and ostentatiously opened her book.

"I'm afraid I'm disturbing you," he said, "I'm sorry. Now there, the airport is on your right and then you need not look at anything more till you get to the Forth Bridge."

She could not help smiling.

"You know Scotland well, I see," said her mother graciously, "yet I think you are English like ourselves."

"And you are perfectly correct, I'm at the university, a failed medical student. I haven't failed quite enough yet to satisfy my father but soon I shall and then I mean to be an artist. I'm on a sketching weekend now — going to Loch Leven; but I won't talk any more, your daughter wants to read in peace. She is your daughter?" he added questioningly.

"Yes," said Roberta quickly, "but people hardly ever believe it." *I really rather like him,* she told herself, *though he is certainly tiresome — now I suppose I must read.* She bent her eyes on her book but found it hard to concentrate, feeling his glance annoyingly fasten on her instead of gazing at her mother — *Which he should be doing, especially if he's an artist,* she thought.

At Dunfermline, which they soon reached, he insisted on helping them out with their luggage and finding a porter for them and very nearly lost his train again.

"What a charming boy," said her mother. "Didn't you think he had a distinct likeness to that portrait of Bonnie Prince Charlie that we saw at Holyrood?"

"Oh, Mother, had Prince Charles white hair, no eye-brows and a scar? Besides, he's English."

"But I expect he's got Scottish blood in him, dear, we all have. And of course he got that scar in the War, and some terrible experience on the battlefield turned his hair white."

"Oh, well, we shall never know about *that*," said Roberta. "We are not likely to be seeing him again ever."

She was wrong on both counts; his appearance was due to a careless experiment in the laboratory at school and this she learned because he turned up at Jimes's guest-house the very next afternoon.

"I decided that what I really wanted to sketch was not at Loch Leven after all, but Dunfermline Abbey; and by a coincidence I believe I am staying at the same guest-house as yourself. I saw the address on your labels."

Roberta did not know whether to be amused or irritated; she decided, or something decided for her, to be amused. The next day he asked if he could make a drawing of her.

"Of me?" she exclaimed, surprised. "Surely you mean my mother, artists always want to paint her."

"Yes, I know, the galleries are full of her, especially in Florence. I shall not add to their beautiful work. It is your face I happen to want."

He worked steadily on the study for a couple of sittings. "It's not bad yet," he then said, putting away his things. "Tomorrow I shall paint it and most probably ruin it. I am really no good at oil portraits. I always work them up too much."

"Then wouldn't it be better to leave it as a drawing?" said Roberta. "I'm no judge but Mother likes it very much."

"Oh, I can't keep off colour," said Charles, "so let's take the bull by the horns in the china shop, as my Uncle Ebenezer used to say."

"Oh," said Roberta, laughing, "have you got an Uncle Ebenezer?"

"Yes, haven't you?" said Charles.

It was at that moment, thought Roberta later, that she had fallen in love with him.

At the end of the first week the Minister of the Kirk which Jimes regularly attended invited the whole party to supper, Roberta, her mother and Charles Curling now being the sole remaining visitors.

"He thinks you are one of the family," said Roberta, "and I didn't undeceive him."

"Thank you," said Charles gravely.

It was an old house with unexpected little steps here and there, one of which led into the sitting-room. Charles, his eyes elsewhere, missed his footing on entering and fell headlong into the room.

"Och, then," exclaimed the Minister's wife, "the poor laddie!"

"Please don't worry," said Charles, picking himself up, "I always come into a room like that," and it was then that Roberta decided that this was the man she was going to marry.

As for Charles, he said he had known that from the moment he met her disapproving eyes in the railway carriage: "Funny eyes they are too," he had added, "yellow rather than brown."

Her engagement met with disapproval from her aunt and uncle, Rollo's parents, who after her father's death had assumed a position of parental care for her.

"You hardly know him, dear," said her aunt, "and you tell me that his parents used to keep a shop somewhere in Yorkshire. I don't know what your father would have said!"

Her uncle was gloomy over Charles's prospects.

"He's very talented," said Roberta, "he's sold some pictures already." (Actually two watercolour sketches to a college friend for £5 each.)

"I dare say," said her uncle.

"He means to teach," said Roberta, "and I have enough for both and we can live at Rowanbank with Mother, of course I don't intend to leave her."

"Well, you have turned twenty-one and are your own mistress, Roberta," said her uncle, "I can't stop you, but at least wait till your Charles has got a job; perhaps he may get his medical degree after all."

He didn't, and his father reluctantly agreed to his transference to an Art course, but his family welcomed Roberta. Her mother, who had taken to Charles from the first for his courtesy and kindness and the romance of his odd appearance, was delighted. They were married as soon as Charles had finished at his art school and a piece of luck had fallen their way in the shape of a teaching post at a school on the coast within easy reach of Rowanbank. The salary, though small, and the beginning of a limited but steady demand for his landscapes, saved his face as a breadwinner in the eyes of their respective families.

"Your mother and I see God's will in this," wrote Charles's devout non-conformist father.

"So that's all right," Charles remarked.

On Roberta's first visit to Charles's home she found herself in a world different from any that she had previously come across, the centre of which was in another dimension.

"God is more real to my father than any of us," said Charles, "not that he doesn't love his children — and, by the way, he'll accept you at once as one of the family — but he feels he must present us spotless before his Maker and as we are far from spotless it is a fearful responsibility."

"And your mother?" asked Roberta.

"Oh, my mother," said Charles, "she's been known to giggle in Chapel. My father ought to have been in the Ministry," continued Charles, "but he was a miner's son.

He left school at twelve determined not to go underground, took an errand boy's job, worked his way up and became the manager of the best ironmonger's shop in the whole district — that's my father."

It was said with pride but Roberta could see that the relationship between the two was not easy. Far worse than his failure to become a doctor was the knowledge that Charles no longer attended Chapel or even church — veiled allusions were made to this and other shortcomings in the extemporary family prayers which, with a reading from the Bible, began and ended the day, and heated theological discussions often followed. Roberta, who was quite un-accustomed to talk on such matters, was uncomfortable and embarrassed, especially when she found herself taken aside first by Charles's father and then by his mother and appealed to to lead Charles back into the fold; they would prefer a Chapel fold but an Anglican one would suffice. Altogether they seemed much more concerned over Charles's and her spiritual welfare than over their worldly prospects.

"If you and Charles make a point of sharing your devotions together as Mother and I have always done, all will go well with you. I shall pray constantly for this," said his father, and to Roberta it sounded almost like a threat.

But his mother said simply, "I shan't be happy in Heaven if Charles can't be there too."

"Why do you tell them what you believe or don't believe?" asked Roberta.

"I couldn't pretend to them," said Charles, "any more than I could to you; and besides I can't hold my tongue. You must know that by this time — why, I couldn't even in the railway carriage."

Roberta laughed. Charles could always make her laugh — that was why she had fallen for him, she supposed. She had needed to laugh so much. She thought probably that

54

Charles's father, that hard-working little boy grown into the serious young man, had needed it too and had found the same relief in his marriage.

Meals with Charles's family were also a new experience, even the food and the times at which it was served were different — there was no alcohol, and lavish midday spreads and high teas replaced lunches and dinners. These were convivial affairs after the long grace was over. Charles was not the only member of the family to be loquacious: his two sisters, both teachers, but deprived of possible husbands by the War, were still based at home and bickered and argued amiably with their father and Charles, but the life and soul of the party was always the mother. After lovingly bustling about till all the cups and plates were filled to her satisfaction, she settled down to enjoy her family. She loved to tease her solemn husband.

"George, you must get your beard trimmed — it's much too long — it's a bad example for Charlie."

"But Charles hasn't got a beard," objected Charles's father, "and you used to like it long."

"Ah, but I loved you then," she exclaimed.

The glance between them, as everyone laughed, remained with Roberta. *That's rare*, she said to herself. *That's what I want with Charles.*

Well, she had had it; not always, of course. There had been times when, had the divorce laws been as they now are, she reflected wryly, she might even have walked out on his maddening inflexibility of conscience and tiresome unworldliness. He never took the least care over his clothes, was abnormally untidy, never bothered what he ate or drank and was dreadfully careless over his health. Equally, of course, he might have left her; heaven knows he had enough provocation at times. But she knew that if they had parted they would have missed a pearl of great price.

55

Now she looked again at the little watercolour she had chosen. Underneath one of those grey slated roofs she had slept on that first visit to Charles's family which had taught her much about the roots from which Charles had sprung. She had been bewildered and uncomfortable from growing pains, but she had also been deeply happy. Each day she had woken to see from her bed a view of the moors that dominated the picture — a beauty so strangely different from her own soft landscape at home but that related to some impregnable sense of security and strength which she knew she had found.

The school holidays had begun and Clare had reconciled herself to the grandfather clock and was pleased to receive a letter from Roberta suggesting that she might like to make a selection of china for herself and Alex: "I have far more than I need or can find room for in the flat and I expect you can do with some additions."

"I should say we could!" said Clare to Alex. "You and the children aren't easy on breakages and chips, not to speak of our guests; but I wonder whenever I can go."

"I think Gran would like it if you took the children with you," said Alex. "It's quite a while since she saw them."

Clare began to look worried. "Wouldn't it be too much for her?"

"I don't think so, she's quite well again now — they probably won't be able to go to Rowanbank much more. If we make it a weekend I might arrange to come too."

Clare's face cleared. "Oh, yes, do," she said. She always felt more at ease with Roberta when Alex was around.

Roberta responded warmly to this suggestion. "Dear Mrs B. has offered extra help," she wrote, "and it will be a real family party — if only Naomi could come too but she has promised to come over later when I shall need her more."

The house was now in agents' hands and the thought that

this might be the last time the expanding flap of the table would be used, the last time she would get out the big table-cloth and the set of handpainted fruit plates that she meant Clare to have, the last time the old schoolroom would be opened up for the children to play in, did not depress her unduly. *Everything has a last time,* she told herself, *so I am not going to allow such thoughts to dampen my pleasure. I mean to enjoy this visit.*

"But what will Boffin do that weekend?" asked Patrick. When they went away for a holiday in the summer they always lent the house, together with Boffin, to one or other of the indigent families known to them through Alex's many involvements.

"Can't Mrs Dent see to him?" asked Alex. Mrs Dent was the latest hard-come-by "Help".

"I don't quite like to ask her," said Clare, "it might frighten her away. I don't think she's fond of cats."

"And she only comes for a little while," said Patrick. "Boffin would be dreadfully lonely, and he'd starve himself — you know he takes ages getting used to people and goes off his food when we're not here."

Bertram, who was either quite callous or deeply sentimental about Boffin, turned down the corners of his mouth, always a danger signal.

"Won't leave Boffin," said Becky gently but firmly.

"Can't he come with us?" asked Patrick.

"Willow hates all other cats," said Clare.

"But Rowanbank's huge," said Patrick, "it's got hundreds and hundreds of rooms — Willow needn't even see Boffin."

"Yes," agreed his father, his eye on Bertram. "I really think that's the best solution if Granny doesn't mind; Boffin can have the run of the attics and a tray."

Although a tray was an affront to his dignity Boffin accepted the situation and settled down comfortably in the Rowanbank attics, where he was visited regularly by Patrick and Becky but never by Bertram, who, however, was no trouble at all on the visit because of Roberta's television.

Clare and Alex had no television, mainly on principle but also because their lives were both so full that they had no time for it. They thought it bad for the children but Patrick had lately taken to paying very regular visits to a school friend. His innocent mother said, "Surely it's time you asked Martin here instead of always going to him," but Patrick had said the children were too much of a nuisance.

Roberta's television set, which she considered an ugly object, lived behind a curtain in an alcove off the sitting-room, an alcove that had once contained her mother's harp which her husband had bought at her request: "So lovely an instrument to look at and the most beautiful of sounds — I really must own one and learn to play it." But the first aspiration was easier to achieve than the second and, after a few not very satisfactory lessons, it was all given up; the harp, still decorative but forever silent, remained in its corner till after her mother's death. Roberta, whom it had always somehow annoyed, sold it to make a convenient space for her newly acquired TV.

The family arrived at tea-time. This was always a proper meal at Rowanbank, not the despicable snack it had often become elsewhere. After consuming paste sandwiches, fruit cake, chocolate buns and a second go of sandwiches Patrick pushed back his chair and sighed with satisfaction. It was good to begin a visit with eating, thought Roberta, especially with children. Now they could be left to themselves up in the old schoolroom to play with the traditional Rowanbank toys that they looked forward to seeing whenever they came — the dolls' house and the Noah's Ark for Becky and Bertram, the fort and the old bound copies of the *Boys' Own Paper* for Patrick. She must somehow find room for these at Coleridge Court — but could she? Well, they would all too soon grow out of them anyhow.

Peace reigned below as the elders chattered together until Roberta, a little maliciously, remarked: "I know you won't mind if I have on my *Gardener's World*; I really mind missing it and I think you'd both enjoy it too."

All eyes then were on "the Box" and no one noticed the door opening slowly or saw Bertram standing in the doorway transfixed. As soon as Roberta switched off he silently vanished. That evening Alex with unusual firmness insisted on Becky and Bertram going to bed at a reasonable hour.

"You mu̱st, or you'll only be overtired and a nuisance to Granny tomorrow and wear her out."

Bertram had made no objection and Clare said hopefully, "Worn out for once."

But this was not the case; on leaving the dining-room after supper everyone was startled to hear violent loud noises coming from the sitting-room, unmistakable gunshots and screams. Hurrying in, they saw Bertram in his pyjamas, sitting entranced before the television alcove, and heard him remark to himself loudly and complacently, "Wish I don't be there, do I!" Before him was depicted a scene of maniac crowds, bloodshed, fire and fury.

"How did he know how to turn it on, I wonder?" said Roberta. That was never divulged; the difficulty was to get him to turn it off throughout the visit.

"Leave him to it," advised Roberta.

"But Alex and I think television so bad for children, Granny," said Clare in her patient voice.

"I know you do," said Roberta, "but we're not talking about 'children', we're talking of Bertram and Becky and Patrick. I don't believe television will do them any harm. As a matter of fact I was going to ask you to take my set off my hands. I can't install that monster at Coleridge Court. I mean to get a little one."

Clare was silent and Roberta went on: "If you have

television yourselves, at least you can keep an eye on what they see."

"But why should they see it at all?" said Alex.

"Don't be foolish, Alex, haven't you noticed how much Patrick seems to know about space-men lately? I really don't think it's quite fair on him and Becky. How do you suppose they feel at school among their friends? Either deprived or dreadfully priggish — it's unavoidable."

"Well," said Alex, after a little pause, "thank you very much anyway for the offer. You may be right; we'll think it over."

Clare knew what that meant: Bertram and Roberta had won again. But she was very pleased with the china. The fruit plates were really lovely and she was able to add to them a set of soup bowls, a good many useful cups and saucers and a big jug and dish of Italian ware in bright soft colours, which she had always admired.

"Isn't there anything you want for yourself, Alex?" asked Roberta. His lack of acquisitiveness always drove her to press him to accept gifts. But it was of no use, he simply smiled and shook his head.

They went off in a loaded car, Boffin glaring from his basket, perched precariously on the top of the television set. After they had gone, the house seemed very quiet and empty; they had had a festive farewell meal and, looking at the children's faces round the big table, Roberta thought of the old flower-seller's cry: "All a growing and a growing and a going and a going."

Well, it's not as if I were off to Australia; and, even if they don't come here again and I can't put them all up at Highgate, I can surely have them for the day — if I've kept enough china. She looked a little ruefully at her depleted shelves. Although she had thought them too large to take with her, she would certainly miss her Italian dish and jug and their loss decided her on the second of Charles's pictures, for if she couldn't have the real objects any longer, then at least she could have them on canvas.

Charles generally preferred to spend his holidays in his native Yorkshire or in Scotland, but this year a fellow artist had tempted him to Italy, to a certain villa a little way out of Siena. "September, that's the time to go, when the peaches and the grapes and the figs all ripen together in the garden here and you can wander among them and pick them at your will and, as you do so, glimpse the towers of celestial Siena from afar." So off they had gone with their baby George for a golden month.

They slept in a spacious stone-floored room with a high ceiling painted with a star surrounded by festoons of flowers; the furniture, pale green, was also painted with flowers and the view, wide and peaceful, extended over vineyards and olive groves to the bare brown Umbrian hills crowned by a white or an orange or a pink farmhouse. They took their breakfast on a loggia, where tiny cyclamen were thrusting up between the stone flags and from where you could indeed see the towers of the city.

Roberta, on her first morning, felt like a child opening a wonderful present. She had never been to Italy before and she had high expectations about art and architecture; in these she was not disappointed, but actually it was the unexpected casual encounters with beauty that delighted her most. No one had happened to tell her of the white oxen peacefully plodding through the centuries, nor of the dazzling blackness of the ilex trees and the cypresses bordering the white roads, nor of the bloom on roofs and walls. These ravished her senses and she felt a little drunk for most of the time.

While Charles was busy with his painting, she and George would lie about in the sun near by, or go for little strolls on their own. George was a placid baby and gave no trouble, unless one counted the crowd of admirers he was wont to attract. All Italians, it seemed to Roberta, were crazy about small children, especially fair-haired, blue-eyed ones. Once, when she and Charles were drinking their coffee on the Campo, with George in his portable pushchair close by, a young workman happened to pass. He stopped, scooped George out of his chair and shouting, "Oop, oop," tossed him up into the blue air as if he were a pigeon. He caught him as he came down and sent him up again, crowing with glee. It had happened too quickly for Roberta to feel fear; by the time she would have done so George was back in his chair and the workman, crying, "Bellissimo bambino," was disappearing into the shadowed calle; but the impression remained of the laughing peasant and the joyful baby, tossed towards the sun.

Another time she left George asleep on a rug at Charles's feet and wandered away towards a small russet-coloured church crouched among a metallic sea of olives. As she got nearer she could hear a thin sound of chanting, and soon she saw a cluster of children on the little piazza outside the church. They were gathered round an old priest who was beating time. It was late in the day, the sun was low and its long level beams shone on the children's dark little heads and black overalls and the rusty figure of the old man, enclosing them all in a glory like the gold background of one of those primitive paintings she had been looking at that morning. She tried to describe it to Charles.

"It's the quality of the light," he said, "the contrasts are sharper here than in England but there is a harmonizing fusion in the light if only I could get it right."

Roberta thought he had got it in the still life that he painted on their last day. Their friend had promised them fruit from the garden and there was an abundance of peaches, figs and grapes, all of which glowed in the picture. They had bought the pottery in the market and the fruit spilled out of the tilted, painted plate — some of the figs were split open to show their purple-pink flesh under the dark green-veined skin and, in the jug, a spray of pointed gothic vine-leaves set off the brilliant autumn flowers.

"Oh, Charles, it's lovely!"

"Third-rate Cézanne," said Charles cheerfully and had wanted to leave it behind; but she rescued it and had it framed and hung.

She had not really looked at it for years; now, as she considered it afresh, she thought that there was enough richness and glow from it to warm her for the rest of her life. She suddenly realized that she had chosen two of her husband's pictures that represented clearly the two contrasting sides of him, the puritan and the artist, and these had never seemed to conflict because they were harmonized always by the humour that, like the Italian sun, fused them into a finely balanced whole.

"So rare, so dear," she said to herself with pride and with pain.

Chapter 6

There were two corner cupboards at Rowanbank — one large and glass-fronted, the other quite small, perhaps a hundred years older, known as the Moses cupboard, with a door painted in colours which had faded harmoniously. It depicted a biblical scene. Pharaoh's daughter, in a full skirt of yellow silk and attended by a page, stood imperiously beside a very blue stream bordered with spiky bulrushes, while Miriam, in peasant costume of green, red and white, lifted a stiff little swaddled Moses from a plaited cradle. In the background Pharaoh's pennanted castle merged into billowy clouds. It was not a work of art but it was unusual and Roberta loved it because it made her laugh and brought again to her the vivid sense of her friendship with Rose at its happiest.

The whole story of that cupboard was pleasant. It had been left to her by an old man whom they had always called Punch — her father's coachman and then his chauffeur. She always thought of him as old but he was probably not so at all when she used to spend hours with him in the stables, which later became a garage. He was a bachelor and fond of children and Roberta loved to show off before him, reciting poems learned from her mother and telling him the stories of Robin Hood and Arthur and the Table

Round, basking in his ready admiration. He lived over the stables and regaled her on peppermint humbugs and curly barley-sugar and when he died she was touched to find he had left her the cupboard in which he had kept the sweets. But then it had been a very ordinary though useful piece of furniture, its door varnished a dull brown, and no one knew anything about Pharaoh's daughter until one day when she and Rose were fifteen years old.

They had been on an expedition together to the zoo, a favourite resort of theirs, and had coasted across London on the open top of a bus — oh, those lovely open buses where, if you were lucky and got the front seats, it was like being in the bow of a ship bounding along the rivers of the streets between the steep banks of houses. It had rained and they had buttoned on the waterproof apron that was attached to each seat. When they got up to rush down the winding stair before being carried on again, the rainwater which had collected in a puddle on their aproned laps tipped over and drenched them and, shrieking with laughter, they had stumbled on to the pavement. At home at last and dry again, they sat before the fire and toasted muffins for tea. The parents were out and they had the house to themselves. Roberta had gone to the corner cupboard for the "squashed-fly" biscuits that they both loved and then Rose had suddenly said:

"There's a chip on the top edge of your cupboard door."

"So there is. I'll have to get it repaired."

"It's a funny blue colour where the varnish has disappeared. Berta, I believe there's something painted underneath."

"Oh, no, there couldn't be," said Roberta.

Opposition always fired Rose. "I bet you anything there is. Do let's try and clean a bit and see."

"What with?" said Roberta, becoming infected as she

often was by Rose's enthusiasm and urge to action.

"Just soap and water and cotton wool might do it," said Rose promptly. "We had a lecture on everything to do with oil painting at our art class at school last term." Of course, Rose would know, thought Roberta as she hurried to fetch what was required.

They started off at opposite corners of the cupboard. "Rub very gently," cautioned Rose. Presently she gave a squeak of excitement. "Blue sky, birds and a cloud — I told you so."

Roberta could hardly breathe from excitement. "Bulrushes and a stream . . . oh, Rose, you are a genius!"

Then Pharaoh's castle and the baby Moses were revealed and they were both silent with emotion.

"It's perfectly splendid," sighed Roberta, when the whole picture had been uncovered, and Rose took hold of her and whirled her round the room, then they both collapsed on to the couch and stared up at the cupboard in admiration.

"I wonder why it was ever varnished over," said Roberta.

"We shall never know, there may be thousands of mystery pictures about — oh, Berta, let's be picture-restorers when we've finished school," said Rose.

"Yes, let's," said Roberta, "darling Rose!"

Their friendship had begun when they were both seven years old. "There's a nice little girl come to live next door," said Roberta's mother, "wouldn't it be a good thing if you and she could be friends? Poor dear, she has no mother so I think we must be extra kind to her."

Roberta was wary of friends chosen for her by her mother and she did not take to Rose at first. She was a thin, rather unattractive child with red corkscrew curls and skirts too short for her and knobbly knees, and she actually still had a Nanny. Roberta's Nanny had vanished when she was six.

"It's because she has no mother," she was told and she

had overheard her mother saying: "I suppose it's her nurse who thinks those awful curls becoming."

"Yes," said her father, "she's an ugly duckling enough with that hair and that queer little pointed face, but you have to look at her twice; and her father tells me she's remarkably clever."

The aura of pathos, combined with the repute of exceptional cleverness, was enough to mark Rose out from the other children Roberta played with and in spite of the Nanny she was impressed by sundry grown-up privileges Rose enjoyed and by a certain mature air that she assumed as a matter of course. For her part, Rose seemed to have decided from the first that Roberta was to be her special friend.

"It's quite unusual for her to take such a fancy to anyone," said the Nanny. "Miss Rose has always liked to keep herself to herself."

This, of course, was ingratiating. Being half an orphan, Roberta thought, had its advantages. Rose was allowed by her father to do much as she pleased and apparently she paid no attention to anyone else. She gained further respect and interest too from certain dark hints she threw out about her mother's death.

"Actually she was poisoned," she confided at last to cement their friendship.

Full of pleasurable horror, Roberta enquired who had poisoned her and why.

"It isn't known, they couldn't discover but everyone knew she'd been poisoned. I heard the doctor say so — he didn't know I was there. I expect it was out of terrible jealousy because she was so beautiful *and* clever," Rose added quickly, in a way that made it clear that she knew that her mother had not been so beautiful as Roberta's, and so she had had to add that bit about her being clever.

But to have had a mother who had been poisoned was

certainly something. "If only she could have been buried in Highgate cemetery with a beautiful monument so that we could have put flowers on her grave it would have been lovely," Roberta said.

Rose agreed, but she was buried in Egypt, which was no good to anyone. Rose had a taste for the macabre — there was that hit she had made as Lady Macbeth at school. This was much later, not at the day school they had attended together but at the big boarding school to which, fired by the stories of Evelyn Sharp and Angela Brazil, Rose had persuaded her father to send her.

"I want to see what it's like for myself," she had said.

Alas, it was not what she had expected. The school, a famous one, was bent on providing for girls an equivalent to the great public schools and it emphasized games and the communal spirit. Rose wasn't good at ball games, having no wish to "play up, play up and play the game", and she wrote miserable letters to Roberta in a vein of lofty self-pity:

No one cares for brains here and you wouldn't believe how stupid and dull they all are. I shall not run away, which I have considered, and I shall not ask my father to take me away, because then they would think they had got the better of me; but I am reading Dante. I made Father let me bring his copy with me — the one with those lovely illustrations, and it must have been prophetic because he is a great comfort to me. I have put all the girls in my house and several mistresses into their appropriate circles in Hell. I have to take it into the lav to read it, because that is the only place in which I can be alone.

Rose was always an omnivorous reader, nothing came amiss and her memory for odd bits of knowledge picked up in her readings was phenomenal. She was too bossy and superior in her manners ever to be popular, but after her success as Lady Macbeth she was treated with respect and there was talk of trying for a university (by no means taken for granted then). But her father died suddenly of heart failure and it was discovered that he had left his daughter very little to support her. She was just eighteen and until she came of age was under the guardianship of an uncle who said university was out of the question.

"What will you do?" asked Roberta.

"I shall train as a cook," said Rose. "A good cook can always get a job. And then I shall go to America and marry a millionaire. You'll marry Rollo, I suppose." Her tone was pitying — she had never got on with Rollo and was undisguisedly jealous of Roberta's affection for him. When they were younger this had taken the form of open hostility. There was the time when she had stuck nails into his bicycle tyres to prevent him taking Roberta on an expedition.

"She's a little vixen, and she looks like one too — mind out that you don't get bitten one day, Bobs. I don't know why you are so thick with her; she'd devour you if she could."

"Oh, well," said Roberta apologetically, "she's Rose; besides she can be awfully interesting, you know."

The truth was that Rose lived her life with a fervour that both fascinated and nourished the more repressed and introverted Roberta. It was perhaps even more tiresome when Rose changed her tactics in adolescence and tried to vamp Rollo, which first amused and then annoyed him, so that sometimes he snubbed her unmercifully. Roberta tried to comfort her but she turned on her.

"I don't care, it's not as if I *liked* him, silly," she said.

But when she heard of his death she threw over her cookery course and came at once to Roberta, who clung to her as someone who belonged to past happiness.

For a period after this, Rose spent all the time she could at Rowanbank and Roberta felt her objective interest in life bracing. She made her read the papers, listen to the news on the wireless and go to concerts and theatres again. In the evenings they played chess, in which they were fairly matched, though Rose was a bad loser. It was something Rollo had always had against her. Roberta was sometimes tempted to let her win. *She minds so much*, she thought with amused wonder, *but I can't do that; it would be like lying to her.*

In all that dark period Rose proved herself the most faithful and loving of friends, but as time went on Roberta began to suffer a sense of unease. Was it that she felt, in spite of all the sympathy, that Rose was too happy? She found herself wanting to argue, to object, to be generally unreasonable and ungrateful.

Rose had finished her cooking and catering course in London and was looking for a post somewhere on the coast — "To be nice and near," she said. "I mean eventually to have a guest-house of my own, of course — now Rowanbank would make a good one, Roberta; there's the lovely garden and it's within easy car-reach of the sea. Don't look so shocked," she laughed.

"What about America?" said Roberta.

Rose laughed again. "That's as may be — we'll have to see, won't we?"

Roberta detected sometimes an assumption that Rose took it as a matter of course that they were to share this undefined future together and that nothing could be better. Why didn't she too feel this wholly satisfactory? The answer ultimately came with Charles. She wrote immediately to Rose about Charles, full of the naïve conviction that the two must like each other because they both liked her, for the experience with Rollo had apparently taught her nothing. The three met together for the first time for lunch at a London restaurant suggested by Rose. Roberta never went to it again.

"You paint landscapes, Roberta tells me," remarked Rose after the introductions were over, "realistic ones of Scotch mountains and cattle." She made it seem an odd, outdated foible.

"Well, yes," admitted Charles, "mountains certainly — not cattle especially. I don't like cattle; they frighten me."

"Do you exhibit much in London?"

"Not really as yet." Charles looked to Roberta for help.

"He's hoping to make contacts in the near future," Roberta said.

"Oh, well, *you* can't help him much over that, can you, Roberta?" said Rose, and turning to Charles she explained kindly: "Roberta knows nothing about art; you must have discovered that by now. I try to get her to come to the most exciting contemporary shows but she much prefers concerts. What do you think of the London group?"

"I'm afraid I'm not familiar enough with their work to say," confessed Charles and was immediately treated to a concise, apt and informative lecture.

"Your friend is extremely well informed," Charles had commented later.

"And you always pretend you know less than you really do," said Roberta, annoyed. "You lay yourself open to people like Rose, you can't blame her."

Roberta had to admit that the occasion had not been very successful but she told herself that restaurants were hopeless places for first meetings. It would be different at Rowanbank. She decided to plan a joint weekend for them as soon as possible.

Meanwhile she pumped Kitty, who happened, at that time, to be seeing a good deal of Rose. Kitty's strong point was not tactfulness, and, besides, she was only a schoolgirl

71

still, but this made her more valuable as a source of information.

"Did Rose say anything to you about Charles?" she shamelessly asked.

"Well, yes," said Kitty.

"What did she say then?"

"Well," said Kitty again, "you mustn't mind, because *I* like him very much."

"Oh, go on, Kitty. I could tell she hadn't taken to him yet, but she will later. What did she say?"

"She said she didn't know how you *could* after Rollo."

"That's pretty ironic of her, I must say," said Roberta.

The weekend at Rowanbank began as the London lunch had ended: in attack and retreat. On the Sunday, however, Rose seemed to be melting and actually proposed a walk with Charles after supper when Roberta said she had letters she must write.

On coming home, Rose seemed cheerful but Charles was quiet, so quiet that as soon as Roberta and he were alone together she said, "Is anything the matter? I hope you enjoyed your walk. Rose seems to have done so."

"She did, I think," said Charles, "she enjoyed telling me that I must accept the fact that I had caught you on the rebound, that I would always be a second best and your heart would always be with Rollo, that you had always belonged to him. She said she thought it would be kinder to let me know how things really were."

"Charles!" exclaimed Roberta. "You didn't believe her?"

"She's very convincing, your Rose," said Charles slowly. "I don't know ... yes, I almost believed her *then*, but I almost don't now." He gave her a searching look and then quickly added, "No, I don't believe her."

She saw that his face had cleared and she now had attention for Rose. "But it was unforgivable of her," she said. "I shall tell her so at once."

"Must you?" said Charles.

"Don't you see that if I don't then this will always be between us?"

She found Rose in the room she always had when she was at Rowanbank and which had come to be known as Rose's room. "Rose, how could you talk such nonsense to Charles about Rollo?" Roberta cried at once. "You know it isn't true."

"I don't know it," said Rose. "Don't shout at me, and if it isn't true, it ought to be. I believe in loyalty if you don't. Do you think I could put anyone in your place ever?"

"That's claptrap," said Roberta, "and, whatever you say, I know perfectly well that you knew you were not speaking the truth to Charles, and will you please go at once and tell him so."

"I shall do nothing of the kind," said Rose. "Good night." She walked past Roberta down the passage to the bathroom.

Has she ever admitted herself in the wrong? thought Roberta furiously. *She's not telling the truth to herself, that's what I can't bear.*

Rose was leaving early the next morning anyway and they hardly spoke to each other before then. They said a conventional goodbye on the doorstep and Roberta had gone back into the house but instinctively she glanced out of the window. Rose was still there standing in the drive, looking back at the house. *Why doesn't she go?* Roberta thought irritably; but she felt miserable that her chief feeling at Rose's departure was relief.

The estrangement lasted on. Roberta, giving herself up to her new happiness with Charles, didn't really bother herself about Rose. *It will come right sooner or later*, she told herself, *and it isn't my fault if she won't tell the truth.*

Her mother said, "Where is Rose nowadays, has she gone to America?" Her memory was slipping away but sometimes stray bits of talk or information would take root and unexpectedly trouble her. Rose had always been particularly good to her mother and on her visits had given up time to amusing and interesting her: "You said once Rose meant to go to America, it was only a joke, wasn't it? Oh, I hope she didn't really mean it."

But she apparently had meant it; for one day, out of the blue, there came a postcard which simply said: "I'm off to the States tomorrow, fearfully rushed and anyway I hate goodbyes. Will write from N. York, Rose." A second card arrived some little time later saying she had found herself a job and loved everything. "Why doesn't she give an address? How maddening of her," fumed Roberta, staring down at the card as if she could conjure one from the blank spaces.

But no address came, nothing came and nearly a year had passed. Her son was born with some difficulty and she was slowly regaining strength after George's arrival when, on a perfectly ordinary grey winter's day with no sort of warning, there was a knock on the door at Rowanbank. *How queer*, thought Roberta, *it sounds like Rose's knock, but it can't be*. Most people used the bell but Rose always had preferred the heavy old knocker, on which she would give a single resounding bang. Roberta flew to the door and there actually stood Rose on the doorstep — an extremely elegant exotic-looking Rose wrapped in white furs with a large bunch of violets pinned to them. Her face was glowing with excitement.

"Yes, it's me, Berta, I'm not a ghost, here catch." She tore the violets from her coat and hurled them at Roberta: "Oh, oh, to see you again, and I'm married to my millionaire, but it's all right, he's not here — can I come in, please?"

Roberta, hugging her, pulled her over the threshold, "Oh, Rose, Rose, you are dreadful. Why, why didn't you tell me, why did you never send me an address? It wasn't kind."

"No," said Rose, "it wasn't, kindness isn't for us."

"And now you've got a millionaire and I've got a baby," said Roberta, her voice trembling. "It's not possible!"

In due time Roberta heard more, but not much more, of Rose's doings. Her job had been in one of the leading hotels in New York and it was there that she had met her husband, who always stayed there on his business visits.

"His name is Vincent P. Primrose — silly, isn't it, for me, being Rose Primrose, but it can't be helped. I don't know what P. stands for — I've never dared ask in case it should be Percy, but I dare say it's just P. Americans have got to have a middle initial, you know, it's the law. He's had two wives before me, one died, one ran off. Yes — he's getting on but I never liked boys and he suits me very well. He travels a lot; he's in the Middle East just now as a matter of fact."

"Oh, dear, I hope it's all right," said Roberta to Charles.

"I shouldn't worry," said Charles, "Rose can look after herself and is doing it very effectively, I should say."

"Now look here, Roberta," said Rose on the third day of her visit, "we may have babies and husbands, but we're still ourselves and I mean to take you away for a break. I've got a week more and you're looking washed out and old."

Roberta immediately felt washed out and old.

"We'll go to London, I think," went on Rose. "It's not as if you wanted country or sea; what you want is a complete change."

Roberta immediately felt that what she wanted *was* a complete change. It had not occurred to her before, but though domesticity with Charles and her baby was wonderful and lovely, of course, it was sometimes a bit weighty.

"Oh, Rose," she said, "I don't think I possibly could. What about baby?"

Rose, who had not shown the slightest interest in

George, now brushed him aside as if he had been a little fly.

"You're not feeding him, thank goodness, so I'll lay on a trained nurse and you can phone every day."

"I'd have to see her first," said Roberta.

"I'll phone today," said Rose. "I know the best place."

"If Charles doesn't mind," said Roberta.

"Heavens, Berta! It's only for a week — after all, I've left my husband for you."

That's quite different, thought Roberta.

But Charles said, yes, she should go by all means, it would set her up.

Roberta had never stayed in London as a visitor before and found it a strange new city — a holiday city, a treat city. Wealth and leisure and freedom from responsibility clothed it in a fresh garment of bright iridescent changing colours. She thought she would miss Charles dreadfully, but she didn't because the whole experience was so unreal, so like an Arabian Night's Entertainment; and because it was so ephemeral she gave herself up to it without reservation. Rose had taken rooms for them at Brown's Hotel.

"I thought American millionaires always stayed at the Ritz," said Roberta.

"I'm not an American millionaire — I'm his wife and English at that, and I've always wanted to stay at Brown's," said Rose.

Every night they went out to the opera, to the theatre, to a concert and all day they talked and laughed, it seemed without stopping, and were as light-hearted and silly and unreservedly happy as they had been in shared treats as children — sillier and happier, thought Roberta, for as children they had not known they were either. Yet for her there was something dreamlike and unreal about this happiness. The two of them exulted together in the ease that wealth ensures. The delightful days were padded with luxury — at the theatres, operas and concerts they had the best seats, they took taxis everywhere — no more bus rides — and Roberta had to stop Rose from buying her everything she admired in the shops.

"You are paying for my keep and transport and tickets," she said, "you must let me keep a little self-respect," and although she was full of amused delight at Rose's clothes and jewellery she was firm in not accepting any of these either. There was a topaz necklace in an antique setting which she especially admired.

"Do have it, Berta, it suits your eyes."

"But you said it was part of your husband's wedding present to you."

"He won't notice it and anyway I chose it," said Rose.

But Roberta wouldn't take it. "You can leave it to me in your will," she laughed.

One day they went to a sale at Sotheby's and Rose bid for some Chinese paintings on silk that Roberta admired. Triumphant when she got them Rose said, "You shall have these too one day." She knew all about Chinese art.

As always, Roberta was continually marvelling at what Rose knew and as always she found her unfailingly interesting. There was nothing to ruffle their relationship and Roberta felt the harmony between them complete and delightful until the last evening.

"I wish this could last for ever," said Rose, "and it could last another week, Berta; that nurse is perfectly adequate for the baby."

"But you've got to meet Vincent in Paris," said Roberta, knowing suddenly that for her part she must now go back to Charles and George at once, that she couldn't be parted from them for even a day longer — that a dream, however lovely and refreshing, was only a dream with no future and that dreams prolonged beyond their proper span go bad on the dreamer.

"He can wait," said Rose. "Do let's stay!"

77

"It's been perfectly wonderful," said Roberta slowly but Rose interrupted her:

"Oh! I can see you don't want to; you can't ever hide anything, Roberta — well, that's that then."

"If you can stay another week," said Roberta, "come home with me to Rowanbank."

"Sorry, no, a hundred times no," said Rose, "but we'll never forget this week, will we? And when I come back we'll do it again, promise!" and Roberta promised.

But, as it turned out, they never did it again and perhaps for that very reason this particular time with Rose was to remain quite distinct and jewel-like in Roberta's memory.

Rose's next visit coincided with the two-year-old George developing a feverish cold. As he was also suffering from a temporary mother-fixation, Roberta would not leave him.

"How you do spoil that child," said Rose, and spent most of her time with Kitty in Highgate.

Next came news of the break-up of her marriage: "It's not his fault," she wrote, "I couldn't deliver the goods; but don't worry, he's been generous and I've got plenty of plans up my sleeve." The plans involved starting up a business of her own, which seemed to absorb her completely for a long period.

"Rose is so fearfully capable," sighed Roberta, "she gets busier and busier, she's always saying she's coming over again but she never comes."

"She's got to make an outrageous success of things first," said Charles, "then she'll come."

But the slump followed and all Rose's energies were absorbed by financial alarms and excursions. Then, just as at last another meeting had been planned, war broke out and "Aunty Rose" became for young George synonymous with parcels containing butter in tins, chocolate, biscuits, packets of dried fruit, tea and coffee and a variety of strange and welcome additions to the healthy, sufficient but boring rationed home diet. Gratefully Roberta acknowledged these parcels and longed for another meeting as soon as life should have become normal again.

The Moses corner cupboard no longer contained squashed-fly biscuits. Instead, among other sentimental relics there was a tin emblazoned with stars and stripes — a tin that had come originally in one of Rose's war-time food parcels. Inside were Rose's letters, all of which Roberta had kept. She took them out now to destroy them — deciding that they must go with so much else of the past. It was silly to have kept it all; what she could remember she would remember and let the rest vanish. The two last letters were on the top of the pile and she fingered them gently — the first that had arrived after the war said she could not after all make it to England but would Roberta *please* come to her — "expenses paid, of course — come *soon*." But Roberta had not gone. Of course, had she known Rose was ill she would somehow have managed it, but since Rose was never ill Roberta had thought it must be her business that was the obstacle. It was just when the twins were expected and so she wrote to say she would go later if it were really impossible for Rose to leave.

"Oh, it wasn't fair not to tell me, it wasn't fair," she had cried afterwards to Charles; but Rose was never fair.

"She didn't want you to go to her from pity," Charles had said, for the next scrap of a letter was enclosed with the topaz necklace and the Chinese silks and the information that Rose had died of cancer the previous month. It said: "I have never loved anyone a quarter as much as I have loved you, Roberta — don't be too sorry about me. I should have loathed being old and I've had a good run for my money."

"I ought to have gone," cried Roberta. "There was that young sister-in-law who could have coped."

"You couldn't have known," said Charles.

79

I never really understood, I was always failing her, thought Roberta as she took out the bundle of letters and replaced the empty tin (it was a good one and might come in useful); though it would probably not have made much difference. As often, when she thought of Rose she felt sad and remorseful, but it suddenly seemed to her that to indulge in such feelings was perhaps a form of egotism.

"And a betrayal of past happiness," she said, apparently to Pharaoh's daughter. She had spoken the words aloud to impress them upon herself, as she shut the door of the little Moses cupboard and entered it on her list.

Chapter 7

The house agent had not been enthusiastic over Rowan-bank. "No central heating and only one bathroom," he commented sadly.

Roberta felt at the same time both apologetic and annoyed.

"We shall, of course, classify it as a fine period house," he said a little more cheerfully.

"But won't that give rather a wrong impression?" suggested Roberta.

He looked at her pityingly.

"The view," she murmured hastily.

He nodded. "Yes, the view is a feature certainly and the garden . . . though a garden, of course, is not necessarily a recommendation these days, Mrs Curling," the house agent told her. "Some people *do* still want one though and there's scope here — well-established flowerbeds and fine trees."

"Well-established too long ago, I fear," said Roberta, "and the trees are not on my ground, you know, in fact there's only the walnut tree actually *in* the garden."

But at the mention of a walnut tree the agent brightened up again. "A walnut tree's a distinct asset," he said. "Well, Mrs Curling, someone may take a great fancy to the walnut tree, you never can tell, but it is probably more likely to attract anyone looking for a place to adapt as a small guest-house or a select private rest-home perhaps, than as a private dwelling."

Roberta felt depressed after this interview; though Alex had warned her that the house might be difficult to sell, she had not at heart believed him. She still hoped to be well settled in Coleridge Court by Christmas, but as the days passed she wondered. It wasn't likely, the agent said, that a sale would be made in the winter. Gradually she steeled herself to the unpleasant business of exposing her home to the possibly critical, necessarily curious gaze of strangers but so far only a few prospective buyers had called to view. These fell into three categories: the first comprised those inquisitive and leisured people for whom house-viewing is a hobby. They were easily identified by their perfunctory attention to details. Roberta resented these. The second category had been misled by the agents' description — "But we want a real period house," they wailed, or: "It will need a great deal spent on it." Towards these she felt apologetic. Then there were the hopefuls who called twice and even took measurements and of these she had at first great expectations, but so far these hopes had faded.

Meanwhile, however, she went stubbornly on with her turnings out and selections. Books! Roberta's heart quailed when she looked at her shelves, for hers had been a book-buying family. Her father, like most educated men of his day, had inherited and added to a fairly extensive library of well-bound classics, novels, biography, poetry and history. Roberta had started her personal collection with the Everyman series, whose price, at one shilling a volume, was within the reaches of her by no means lavish pocket money. There they were — children's stories in blue, fiction in red, essays and histories in brown and poetry in green. Inside each of them was printed:

"I will be with thee to be thy guide
In thy most need to be by thy side."
And so they had been and she was not going to forsake
them now. How well their stout bindings and good paper
and print had stood up to the test of time, whereas her
paperbacks, so many years younger, were mostly tattered
and torn. She recalled her father's contempt for paperbacks
— "Continental Flimsies" he had called them, for they were
scarcely ever seen on British shelves until the Penguins and
the Pelicans came to roost there — not before they were
needed, she admitted, with the price of hardbacks soaring
after the Wars.

Gradually every shelf in the house had become un-
comfortably crowded. Roberta continually made vows to
buy no more books, but she never kept them. Now,
however, she must bring herself to select the limited
number she would have room for in future, but how could
she begin this miserable task? Her prime favourites she
almost knew by heart, and though she hardly needed to
reread them, it was unthinkable not to give them shelf
space. Then there were certain classics which could not in
all decency be left behind and there were all those authors
who had been milestones in her development at different
stages in her life: Samuel Butler, for instance, and D. H.
Lawrence and H. G. Wells — she doubted whether she
would ever open them again, yet she knew that once parted
from them she might want them desperately, in fact so
much so as to force her to replace them. Oh, it was
hopeless, yet it must be done. The first thing she decided to
work out was which shelves she could take and calculate
how many books and of what sizes they would hold.
Unfortunately those in her father's study library were too
tall to fit into Coleridge Court and in the sitting-room
there were alcoves with fixed shelves. There was a sizeable
glass-fronted book-case in the hall that she must have, and

she thought she could squeeze in one other. There were two possibilities both now in her bedroom, one was elegant, prettily shaped and finished but flimsy, and she thought that in any case she would have chosen the plainer but better made and more serviceable shelves, even had these not also had associations which made them something other than mere pieces of furniture. They had been made by her son George as the occupation of his last school summer holidays — the summer of the fall of France and the Battle of Britain.

She was lying on the lawn in the garden listening to a robin, and also to the distant vibration of guns across the channel which, on fine clear days, you could feel rather than hear in that part of Kent. She thought there had never been a robin's song sweeter but poignancy was an added quality to beauty of every kind in that precarious summer, a sharpness and sweetness, a heightening of all pleasurable experiences. It was a golden late September afternoon and besides the guns and the robin, she could hear bees in the Michaelmas daisies and George's saw busy at his carpenter's bench in the stables. But presently another sound invaded her ears, the tiresome familiar whine of the air-raid sirens — "blest pair of Sirens", Charles called them. Soon, looking up, Roberta saw aeroplanes, a bunch of them swooping at each other in the clear sky, too far away as yet to be real. Near her the swallows were darting and swooping in imitation. She watched the planes lazily, but presently they grew nearer and bands of black smoke wove in and out of the white.

"Come along, George, we'd better take shelter. They seem to be coming this way," she called. "Here comes Father with the dogs."

They all went down into the Rowanbank commodious cellar, now fitted out quite comfortably for day and night accommodation. The spaniels, Gog and Magog, barked a little in protest.

"They must think us quite mad," said Roberta.

"Well, we are, aren't we?" said Charles.

George looked at his father solemnly. "We're not at all mad, I think," he said. "You said yourself the other day it was the only sensible thing to do."

Roberta sighed; she found it strange that Charles of all people should be the father of the literal-minded, practical George, but her musings on the tricks of heredity were interrupted by the clatter down the steps of the old and young William Baxter and Joe Smith, a fellow farm-worker. The fighting now was directly overhead and there was the loud noise of planes descending. They were silent until the sound faded.

"Just hope none of ours came down," said old William. "We can't spare 'em."

"Why don't those bloody Americans come in, I'd like to know?" said Joe. "We could do with some of their gangsters over here."

"Yes, but how to get rid of them afterwards?" said William. "Finish the job by ourselves, that's what I say."

The all-clear sounded soon, and they emerged again; the robin was still singing. George picked up a bullet from the doorstep and put it in his pocket.

"If you've nothing better to do," he said to young William, "be a good chap and bowl to me for a bit." The season was over, but George was loath to put his bat away and the practising nets were still up in the home field.

Roberta was wondering if the enemy planes had been turned back or had reached London again. She sickened at the thought. The sight of George putting on his pads was comforting. "You're like Sir Francis Drake, George," she said.

85

"Who?" said George. "Oh, wasn't he the Johnny who discovered America?

"No," said Roberta, "he sailed round the world but when the Armada was sighted he went on to finish his game."

"Well, it couldn't have been cricket," said George, "for that wasn't played then."

"It was bowls," said Roberta.

"Oh, bowls," said George in disgust. "Why did you say it was cricket then?"

"I didn't," said Roberta — but he was off. If only he was interested in something besides cricket and carpentry, she thought. Charles had gone off to do his Home Guard duty and she brought out some sewing to do in the garden.

She felt impelled to spend as much time out of doors as possible, she supposed it was because she was suffering from a sort of claustrophobia from having to resort so frequently to the cellar. She could now hear the familiar sound of ball on bat coming up from the meadow, a singularly reassuring and homelike sound, and she felt a rush of love and pride in the village and all the people in it who were sharing their fears and hopes, joys and sorrows as never before. *There must be less loneliness about now than there has ever been*, she thought; *it is quite different from the last war because now we are all in it together. How adaptable we are. I would not have believed, for instance, that I could get so used to danger; not that I'm not still afraid, but I'm no longer panicky.* She looked back over the short months since France had fallen. *Then* she had felt desperate, had tried to get George away to friends in America, only he had refused to go, had herself contemplated leaving Rowanbank and, with Charles migrating to Devonshire, only he refused to go.

What had changed her? She believed it was simply Churchill's speeches. Yet she had not been before much of an admirer of his, almost the reverse; but yes, his words, just his words had changed her whole mood, and not even directly heard but coming over the air as they all sat round the wireless — such could be the power of the right words at the right moment, spoken in the right way. It had completely amazed her. Afterwards, of course, the confidence the words brought had been reinforced by the successes in the air of the "few". That confidence was still growing but, although she was no longer in a state of terror, she was often very tired from the constant loss of sleep and the deep-reaching loss of security.

Sometimes, if tired enough, she managed to sleep through the noise, especially since they had moved their beds down below; she thought she would do so tonight for she had been to London the day before and was unusually exhausted. There had been a bad raid and the train journey had been circuitous and protracted and when she reached her destination at last it was through an indirect route past streets cordoned off and the rubble of ruined buildings. The air had been full of sour smells and tiny floating bits of charred paper. She took ages to get to the National Gallery where she was meeting Kitty and nearly missed the lunchtime concert; but, oh, the relief of Myra Hess playing Beethoven to the rapt grateful audience that had collected in the basement, clutching their sandwiches and gulping their coffee! And afterwards there was the picture to see — the one treasure which, selected out of the whole collection and changed at intervals, was displayed in the entrance hall in solitary splendour. The last time she was there it had been a Claude, prince of escapists, this time it was Chardin's bottle of wine and loaf of bread. Roberta thought how seldom she had seen a masterpiece isolated from its fellows, neither supported nor diminished by them, and the impact made the more direct and memorable as a result. This particular picture, in its profound selective simplicity, seemed to be conveying some message to her; it was demanding a reappraisal of her values.

She had some business to do after the concert and then there was the long uncertain journey home. An air raid held them up about half-way; the train slowed down and stopped and everyone in her carriage began to talk.

There was an anxious lady who was afraid she should miss her station — "They call them out, I know, but it's difficult to hear sometimes. Won't it be nice when the names go up again? I've got to catch a bus from the station, but do you think it's safe to go in a bus?"

"Safe as houses," said a man and they all laughed. "Well, you see, once the bus has started you won't know you're being bombed."

A porter came by with a megaphone: "Germany calling the British Isles," he called out, imitating Lord Haw-Haw, and everyone laughed again.

"I've got the last peppermint creams in the country here," said a girl. "Have one," and she passed them round, but no one took one — generosity could go too far.

"Save 'em for the kids," said the man.

Then they went on again but it was very late before Roberta got home.

Now she let her work fall into her lap and closed her eyes. She awoke to see George coming up the garden path towards her.

"I'll finish those shelves tomorrow, Mum," he said. "I promised I'd get them done by the end of the holidays."

"They've flown — it always seems the end of the holidays," said Roberta.

She began slowly to sort out the volumes on George's bookshelves. As she did so she could see back through the years the figure of her schoolboy son, but with a pang she realized that she could no longer remember his features clearly; as a baby, yes, but beyond childhood — faceless. If only she had had more opportunities to know him, but his

88

prep and public schools had robbed her of time. She sat and mourned for what she had lost and for what she had never had. George's education had been generously paid for by her uncle, Rollo's father, and he had gone to the schools he had advised, for Charles and she had been quite hard up. Also, because George was an only child they had thought it better for him to go away. But now she wondered. Immediately after school the Army had swallowed him up. He was old enough to come in for the end of the War and after it was ended he remained in the Army, which seemed to suit him. He made an early marriage to a girl in the WAAFs — the Women's Auxiliary Air Force — and Roberta had not had time to get to know his young wife properly either. A drunken driver on a wintry road had seen to that and then she had become a substitute mother to their two babies, who were now nearer and more real to her than George. When she dreamed of her son, as she sometimes did, his personality merged into that of Alex; it was as if he had ceased to exist for her in his own right.

Chapter 8

And yet they were not at all alike. George she remembered always in relation to some object: a cricket bat, a football, a saw, a bicycle, a gun, a car. Alex she saw as a figure in a void. Even as a little boy he seemed lacking in the common acquisitive factor.

"What do you do with your pocket money?" she had once asked him curiously.

"He mostly gives it to me," said Naomi.

"Then you shouldn't let him."

"But I need money so much more than he does," expostulated Naomi.

"Alex has too big a bump of altruism," she complained to Charles. "I don't know how he'll manage in life; he'll never dream of feathering his own nest. I doubt if he'd recognize a feather if he saw it."

Well, after all, he hadn't done so badly — it is seldom the things we worry about in the future that prove to be the real trials. He was good at his job and people liked him, though she suspected that they thought him an odd fellow; but they trusted him, just because he so queerly didn't want to feather his own nest first and foremost, and Clare saw to it that he didn't give quite all the pocket money to his causes. Patrick was turning out to have inherited George's practical turn, which was a comfort.

The phone rang. Roberta got up from the floor, where she had been kneeling to read the titles on the lower shelves, and saw that her hands were covered with dust. *That just shows,* she thought ruefully, *I'm afraid Kitty was right, I am letting things go. Heaven knows when all my shelves last had a proper spring cleaning.*

It was Alex on the phone. "How often that happens," exclaimed Roberta.

"What happens?"

"I was thinking of you and then you rang."

"Oh," said Alex, "then I must think of too many people, Clare says the phone's always at it. Well, anyway how are you getting on?"

"Not too well," said Roberta, rashly, as she afterwards acknowledged. "I've begun to try and tackle the books. I never dreamt there were so many; they are all over the house besides the study."

"Yes," said Alex, "Clare was saying she thought they'd be a problem. Now, Granny, she and I have had a good idea." Roberta steeled herself.

"You remember Clare's cousin Morris, don't you? He's just retired from his librarian's job and he's at a loose end and we're sure he'd be very glad to come and help you. He knows all about books. He could list them for you and that would make it a much quicker business for a valuer — you'll be selling nearly all of them, I suppose."

"I suppose so," said Roberta sadly, and paused. She did indeed remember cousin Morris, a great talker, one who told you in detail about many things in which you were not interested. She supposed that if he were to list her books she would have to have him to stay, perhaps for some days. She quailed at the thought.

"It's very considerate of you both, my dears," she said at last, "but really I can manage quite well if I take it slowly."

91

"But why should you tire yourself out unnecessarily? Anyway, you don't quite know how much time you can allow yourself, do you, dear? A buyer may turn up any day and besides you'll be doing a really good turn to Morris; he'd love to be of use."

"Well, I'll think it over," said Roberta. "Are you sure there aren't any books you want for yourself? You didn't look at them much when you were here. At least take some for the children — I'll put some aside."

"None for me," said Alex firmly. "I get all I want from the library; but I'll run down soon again and we'll see about the children. And let us know soon about Morris, won't you?"

"Very well," said Roberta, "it'll be lovely to see you." She rang off rather abruptly.

It was typical, she thought, both annoyed and amused, for Alex could never resist a good turn and if he could bring off two at once was really happy. If she let Morris come it would probably be quite difficult to get rid of him. She was also conscious of the fact that she disliked the idea that Alex and Clare thought the job of dealing with the books too much for her. This decided her on walking to the village and back to see about some packing-cases she wanted to order from old Benson, the carpenter. It was the longest walk she had taken since her fall and, feeling tired on the way back, she turned aside to rest on a favourite seat in the churchyard, her mind busy with the problems of finding a good reason for declining Morris's help. The good reason was miraculously at hand.

Roberta had a weakness for churchyards. It was one of the attractions of Coleridge Court that it was close to old Highgate churchyard, through which she and her friend Rose and little Kitty used to walk together to school. They each had their favourite among the tombstones. Hers was a large family one — all those children, one after the other, fascinated her: John and Edith, Alfred and Frederick, Maria

92

and Henry, Florence and Alice, Hester and Arthur and baby Samuel. She pictured all the children sitting at a huge dining-table with the father, John William, late of this Parish, at one end, and Edith, beloved wife of the above, at the other. Rose favoured an earlier headstone with a skull and crossbones carved on it and Roberta remembered Kitty, who always lagged behind, calling out suddenly: "This is mine — oh, Berta, look! This one didn't die at all, she just fell asleep." Death was too far away, too alien to cast any shadow over the three little girls among the tombstones and even now the elderly Roberta at the back of her mind still thought of a churchyard as peopled with a quiet assembly of peaceable companionable folk. She never felt lonely in one and this village churchyard was a pretty place, well kept, with all its flowers of love bright upon the calm graves.

Thinking these thoughts, she felt put out by seeing her seat already occupied by a man, a stranger who, stretched out on it, was apparently dozing in the sun; but she was not going to give up her rest. She coughed. The man opened his eyes and at once made room for her. He was rather shabbily dressed — *But that means nothing nowadays*, she thought — a middle-aged man, rather good-looking, though he had boot-button eyes of that sort of opaque blackness which is singularly inexpressive.

"Good morning," he said, and his voice was educated and pleasantly pitched. "You caught me napping — it is so peaceful here. There is nothing like an English country churchyard for peace, is there?" As she sat down, he gave her a quick glance, smiled and continued.

"Beneath these rugged elms, that yew tree shade,
Where leaves the turf in many a mouldering heap
Each in his narrow cell forever laid
The rude forefathers of the hamlet sleep."

Roberta started, the quotation fell in so aptly with what

93

she had been feeling, it was spoken sensitively too.

"Oh, yes," she responded, "the 'Elegy'. I often think of it myself here. The elms all gone, alas! But the yew is still with us and the forefathers, of course." Then she added with some hesitation, although they seemed to have made friendly contact so naturally, "You are fond of poetry?"

He laughed, "I set out to be a poet once but I found I wasn't one, so I made it my stock in trade instead: poetry and other books. I had a bookshop — until quite recently, in fact."

Again Roberta gave an inward start. She prided herself on a sensible view of life; coincidence, she held, was just chance, not "sent" or "meant" or whatever fanciful people like her mother liked to take it for. But there did seem something unusual, to say the least, in this meeting; first that quotation chiming in so exactly with her mood and now a book business. Her mind raced on, could it be that this stranger was the very excuse she was looking for to confound Alex and Clare?

She found herself asking all about his shop and hearing that it had been in Folkestone but now was no more. He had knocked about the world a bit, he said, but then wanted to settle down and had sunk all his capital in this shop in partnership with a friend.

"We were at school together and had scarcely met since. It was bad luck for me running across him again because, as it turned out, he was no good, a gambler who had cleared off with all he could lay his hands on, leaving nothing but bad debts. Oh, well! That's how it is. I'm sorry to bore you with my troubles but you asked for it, you know. My old car's broken down and I just dropped in here to look at the church while the garage is patching it up, but it's locked up."

"Yes," said Roberta, "we've had vandals."

"You can't trust anyone nowadays," said the stranger.

94

Roberta had liked both his frankness and his lack of self-pity.

"You can get the key at the Vicarage," she said.

"It's rather late now," he said, "I'd better be pushing off. Well, it's been a pleasure to meet you."

And then Roberta heard herself saying, "But you know, it is rather extraordinary, meeting you here just now, I mean," and she began to tell him of her move and how the worst problem was the books. Now she wondered whether, knowing about them as he did, he could recommend anyone who could list and value her books for her.

"Arnold Hathaway," said the stranger with a little bow, "that's the fellow for you, at a loose end this very week and at your service. I could come over tomorrow if you liked and have a preliminary look at them anyway."

Roberta went home a little breathless but elated. She had of course hoped that he might offer to come himself. Arnold Hathaway — an unusual name and a pleasing one she thought, with two poetic associations. She had definitely taken to the man and hoped that evening that it wasn't all a dream and that he would actually turn up as arranged.

He did so, arriving at the time fixed and, after having looked round, said the listing and valuation would take about three days. He gave her the phone numbers of two references and having named what seemed to her a very reasonable quotation for the job, proposed, if she were satisfied, to begin the very next day. After he had gone Roberta made two phone calls, the first to a Folkestone doctor for the reference, which was satisfactory. *I shan't bother about the second one*, she thought and rang Alex.

"There's no need to trouble Morris," she said, "I've found someone locally," well, that was nearly true, "who is experienced and not at all expensive. I think it's really better to have it done professionally, Alex."

"Oh, very well," said Alex, "if you've made up your mind, though Clare will be disappointed. Who is this chap?"

"You'd approve, dear, he's down on his luck — a bankrupt bookseller but it's not his fault. He's a nice man and he loves poetry." *I sound just like Mama*, she thought suddenly and rang off.

"I can't think who this fellow can be," said Alex to Clare afterwards, "she never mentioned him before but she seems absolutely decided."

"Then there's nothing to be done — you know your grandmother," said Clare. "Bertram, if you go on hugging Boffin so tightly he'll scratch you."

"No, no," said Bertram. "He's a good cat, he's a nice cat." A moment later he dropped Boffin with a loud roar.

"What did I tell you?" said Clare.

Bertram stopped roaring in mid-yell. "No, no," he said in his ordinary voice, "it was a naccident, he thought I was a tree."

Clare, annoyed at Roberta's summary dismissal of her cousin, and struck again by a certain resemblance between her youngest and his great-grandmother, said with an unusual firmness:

"It *wasn't* an accident, Bertram, he scratched you because you were squeezing him."

"A very normous tree," said Bertram.

Roberta, at the end of Arnold Hathaway's first day's work, was well pleased with her bargain. He had arrived punctually and had seemed to know his job. He had at once picked out some rare editions from her mother's collection of poetry.

"Yes," said Roberta, "my father delighted in procuring these for her — this little Donne, for instance. Are you interested in this?"

"Indeed, yes," said Arnold Hathaway.

They had a pleasant lunch together. He was a good

raconteur and had travelled widely. Roberta congratulated herself that it was not Clare's boring cousin sitting opposite her. She had opened up the dining-room for his benefit (when alone she took her meals in her sitting-room) and he admired her view and was enthusiastic over her Georgian candlesticks and other silver.

"Forgive me," he said quite anxiously, "but I hope you have these valuable pieces well insured. I came across a case only the other day of carelessness in that respect and in these degenerate times thefts are so deplorably common."

She reassured him.

The second day they discussed their favourite authors; he confessed to an unfashionable liking for eighteenth-century poetry, "Including the Churchyard School," he said, smiling.

Roberta found him most knowledgeable. That afternoon she had visitors who stayed late and she was not surprised that, by the time they left, Mr Hathaway's old car had disappeared from beside the dining-room french window where she had told him to park it. She glanced into the study and saw the neat lists lying on the table. *I shall quite miss him when he has finished*, she thought.

But the next morning he did not turn up and, rather put out at receiving no explanation, she went to lunch alone in the dining-room. There she found her explanation. What she did not find was the Georgian candlesticks, nor the cream jug, nor the salver, nor any of her spoons. The note Arnold Hathaway had left she read with incredulous horror. It said:

Dear Mrs Curling,

You have been very kind to me, I have enjoyed our talks and I am sorry to have to take your silver but my need is greater than yours. It was indeed a happy chance that brought me to your churchyard, where I was feeling

97

so desperate when you found me that I actually wished myself with our rude forefathers beneath the sod; but your silver should save the situation. You see, it is a case of exchanged identity, such as was dear to the heart of the Elizabethan dramatists. My tale was true but it is my partner who is Arnold Hathaway and I am the bad lot and the gambler. I have nearly finished your inventory and you will not find any of your books missing, though I was sorely tempted to slip that little Donne into my pocket. Why I didn't, I don't quite know — perhaps you do. I don't much care for my own name so will once more borrow one.

"Autolycus"

As a child Roberta's worst dreams were of familiar and loved faces suddenly turning into mocking masks: the ultimate horror of any frightening fairy story was that of the witch or wizard or wicked stepmother disguised as a harmless peasant or beautiful Queen. Now her first reaction to this outrageous letter was not anger but a bewildered fear. Trust was betrayed and the foundations of a bearable world trembled. But she must ring the police. She had little hope, however; the thief had had twenty-four hours' start and was no fool — of that she was sure. Not that this excused her for being his dupe. Fury with herself now possessed her. How could she have been so credulous! She admitted with shame that it was more to get a rise out of dear good Alex and Clare than to escape Morris that she had leapt at this rascally stranger. She must indeed humble herself before them now and the worst of it was that they would be so kind. She was right.

"Don't mind so much, Granny," Alex said, "don't blame yourself so. I've been taken in many a time; but, you know, I think that's better than never taking a risk with people."

"Yes, Alex," said Roberta sadly, "for you it may be. I can't feel like that. You see, it's like robbing you and Clare."

"Oh, Georgian silver doesn't really fit our way of life," said Alex, "so don't worry about that."

She felt still more humbled as she put the receiver down. It was a relief to be scolded thoroughly by Kitty and to be able therefore at last to find excuses for herself.

"But, Kitty, he really did like poetry, I'm sure of that. I think that's why he didn't take the Donne or any of the other books. He respected my liking it too; but, oh, how *could* anyone who loves Grey's 'Elegy' have stolen my silver?"

"Well, Hitler loved Beethoven and I dare say Nero played the fiddle quite well, and how many great poets and painters have been unfaithful to their wives — tell me that."

Roberta acknowledged once more to herself that the marriage of Heaven and Hell was an inescapable fact and it then seemed to her that the foundations of the world were steadying again. She had thought the "Elegy" would be spoilt for her but this was silly. Its beauty was undimmed. Light remained light and darkness darkness, though here on earth so often interwoven. There was one thing, however, that she would have liked to have known. If her silver had not been insured would it have affected Mr Hathaway? (She still thought of him by this name.) He had enquired so anxiously about this. She was very much afraid it would not, though she believed that he might have sincerely regretted it.

As she had feared, the police failed to trace the thief or her things. She grieved now over the personal loss — it was their vanished beauty, not their value that she minded and missed. Charles would have understood this but she thought he might have done what no one else did. He might have laughed. The thought of his possible amusement chased away bitterness. After all, she reminded herself, she had always had a soft spot for Autolycus and if this were not simply sentimentality it ought not to harden when she herself was a victim. It occurred to her too that really she had little or no right to the silver herself, for she had neither worked for it nor particularly deserved it and it was probably true that Mr Hathaway's need was greater than hers. "To each according to his need," and, though of course she knew theft was wrong, somehow a little of Alex's attitude to possessions seemed to have rubbed off on her. It no longer appeared a matter of life and death which of them she should keep. "Lay not up for yourselves treasures upon earth where moth and rust corrupt and where thieves break through and steal." She suspected, though, that she might not be able to feel like this for very long, and meanwhile the practical necessities of the move must be attended to. Certain treasures, whether rightly or wrongly, had been acquired and were her responsibility and must be dealt with. She must continue with her lists.

Piano, she wrote down firmly, for, although it was seldom used and she knew the Village Hall was badly in need of one, she was not prepared to give up the piano.

Chapter 9

She always thought of it as Naomi's piano for they had bought it when, with the realization that the child had undoubted aptitude, music for the first time had entered seriously into the family. The old Broadwood, with its pleated green silk behind the fretwork and side brackets for candles, upon which her grandmother had entertained the gentlemen after dinner with Mendelssohn and Chopin and the less difficult Beethoven sonatas, was not good enough for a budding genius. For so Roberta held her granddaughter to be, from the time when she had picked out melodies by ear at an early age, on through the steady accumulation of certificates and prizes right up to that unlucky journey to Salzburg. Indeed, she still did so, and cherished a secret hope that it was yet not too late for Naomi to make a comeback and to establish her preordained fame as a solo pianist.

How thrilling it had been, that triumphant progress — almost without any setback, unless that rather difficult phase at the beginning of adolescence was to be counted, when the child had flagged a little and seemed to find the required practising wearisome. How to cope with this had been one of the few disagreements between herself and Charles.

"I think it's a mistake to put pressure on," he had said.

"But, Charles, she must practise if she is to do well in her next exam — it's crucial."

"Does it really matter all that much?"

"Of course it matters. Everyone knows there's so much competition nowadays."

"Pressure was put on me, if you remember, and little good it did."

"That was *quite* different. You never wanted to be a doctor, you weren't meant to be one; it was your father who wanted it."

"And don't we want this for Naomi?"

"Of course!" Roberta had cried, stamping her foot with irritation. "But only because it's obvious it's what she was made for, what she herself wants more than anything."

"Perhaps you are right," Charles had said, "it's difficult to tell with Naomi."

This was true. As a child Naomi did not easily or often show her feelings. Where Alex was exuberant she was withdrawn — he hugged, she submitted to being hugged, escaping as soon as possible. When, on one occasion, Roberta had to leave the children, he had cried: "I can't bear you to go away, Mummy, my life is wasted without you." Naomi, on the other hand, was silent or, very occasionally, to Roberta's intense gratification she might mutter: "When shall I see you again?" Anyone she disliked she ignored quietly but firmly. She seldom cried and she did not laugh often, though she seemed happy enough. She had been a delicate child and Roberta had fussed over her and adored her as a rare little creature never to be taken for granted. Her reserve only intensified a certain quite pleasurable unease in the relationship. If she had ever analysed her feelings for the two children she might have said that she loved Alex but was in love with Naomi. She was not, however, jealous of Franz. No, it was not for being Naomi's husband that she found it hard to forgive him but because she held him to be the cause of her forsaking her career — and no talk either of any children yet to compensate, and she dared not ask about this or even hint, for fear of giving offence.

Naomi had not wanted to have the piano sent out to Austria. Franz had a Bechstein grand and it would have been superfluous and a needless expense. So it remained at Rowanbank and sometimes when she was sure no one could hear her Roberta would stumble over a tune or two, regretting now that she had not kept up her music; but it had seemed unnecessary when Naomi was at hand to play so infinitely better than she ever could hope to do.

It was not strange that with her head full of the piano and its associations she should dream that night that she was playing it, not in her natural floundering fashion but as brilliantly as her granddaughter. In fact she was performing to a crowded and spellbound audience, at the Royal Festival Hall, it seemed. What was strange was that when she woke the music continued.

Opening her eyes, she saw the sun glimmering and shimmering through the leaves of the walnut tree to the sound of Mozart. She sprang out of bed as if she were young still and nearly fell because, strangely, she was old. Throwing a wrap round her, she went downstairs and there was Naomi at the piano.

"Darling, how lovely!" she exclaimed. "But why didn't you let me know? I didn't expect you till later on in my proceedings."

"Franz had a conference in Paris and we thought it would be nicer if we were both away together and I didn't think it would matter to you when I came. I can help with the clearing out now, can't I?"

"Indeed you can, but how did you get here at such an early hour?"

"I came by a night flight and I hired a car at Heathrow —
I've got it for the week, they're not expensive if you drive
yourself and I thought it would be handy — I want to get
about a bit, see Clare and Alex and so forth." Roberta's
heart sank a little. *Only a week and visits to be paid*, she thought,
but immediately rebuked herself. Naomi was here now in
the present moment and that was joy enough.

"You're looking well," she said. Naomi had too narrow a
face and her features were too irregular for beauty but she
had large very clear grey eyes which, when they were lit by
interest or emotion, looked even larger from the thinness
of the face and gave it a luminous quality which was very
attractive. Her smiles came rarely but when they came
they were delightful.

She smiled up at her grandmother now and said: "So do
you. I hope I didn't disturb you; I thought you were usually
up and about by now. I called in at the cottage and got a key
from Mrs B."

"I'm afraid I've let myself get into bad habits of sleeping
late," said Roberta. "I can't get off easily; I suppose it's
having so much on my mind with the move."

"Yes," said Naomi, "it must be a great upheaval for you.
You go and dress and I'll get us some breakfast."

After breakfast Roberta went to phone Kitty, who had
been coming for the weekend. She had no intention of
sharing Naomi's precious time with anyone else.

"Why didn't she tell you she was coming, the inconsiderate little toad?"

"She's not really inconsiderate, Kitty, it's only that her
margin of communication is low."

"Well, it comes to the same thing. Yes, of course I
understand and, yes, I can and I will put off my visit and,
yes, I *do* know Naomi's perfect."

Roberta put down the receiver abruptly. Kitty never
appreciated either of the grandchildren properly — a form

of jealousy, Roberta supposed; but she forgot Kitty as soon as she got back to the sitting-room.

With Naomi's arrival the house had come alive again and the hours flew past. Together they set about tackling drawers and cupboards, an exhausting but no longer a grim task done in company. Naomi shared Roberta's love of order and they made separate heaps of oddments: one for village jumble, one for Oxfam, one for a bonfire and one to keep for Coleridge Court. She was not allowed to linger, as she would have done if alone, over the seductive boxes of family photographs and letters, old theatre programmes, school reports, all the flotsam and jetsam of the past. Naomi was ruthless.

"What a hoarder you are, Mother," she said.

"It's having had so much room," said Roberta, sighing.

"Well, let's get on — what shall we do with these old cameras?"

The weather behaved perfectly. At first it rained steadily, the insistent slanting drops beating against the windows, cutting them off from the outside world which indeed ceased to exist for Roberta. Then, when the back was broken of their allotted tasks, the still-warm October sun shone out so brilliantly that they took their lunch outside to the old summerhouse among the rampant sprawling Michaelmas daisies.

"Are you sure there is nothing that you want to take back with you?" asked Roberta a little wistfully.

"Well," said Naomi, "perhaps some of my old children's picture books — Johnny Crow and the Beatrix Potters and the Caldicott Rhymes. There was a pile in the Nursery: I thought they would have all gone to Alex."

"He had his own old ones for the children, I kept yours separate," said Roberta, her pulse quickening. She at once saw an entrancing picture of Naomi with a book and a baby on her lap.

But Naomi went on: "You know I work two days a week now at Franz's Children's Clinic and I thought they would like them — the pictures are so good and I could easily translate the text for them."

"No, you never told me," said Roberta flatly. "Do you enjoy that?"

"Oh, yes, and I'm thinking I might take a course next year so that I could be of more use. By the way, now we've got on so well with the turning out I think I shall run down and see Alex and Clare and the children, tomorrow perhaps. I'd better give Clare a ring now and see if it's convenient. Then I might spend a night in London."

"Very well," said Roberta. She sat on alone, holding on her lap a box of her mother's kid gloves, yellowing with age and with tiny pearl buttons. They seemed as melancholy as the little ghosts of white roses nipped by the early frosts that hung over the summerhouse roof. "Working at a clinic and about to take a course" — why did Naomi take up these things with which she had no business and why did she mention them so casually and not even talk them over with her? How little time there was left for talk now anyway, for she must send her off to Alex and Clare with a smile tomorrow, Roberta supposed.

"And like a sad slave stay and think of nought,
But where she is, how happy she makes those.
So true a fool is love that in her will
Though she do anything he does no ill."

She repeated the lines to herself partly for comfort and partly in admonition.

Naomi came bounding back over the lawn, looking amused. "It's all right for tomorrow, Clare says, but it seems that Becky keeps on and on about wanting a clock from you for herself, since Patrick is getting the grandfather . . . Clare's afraid she suffers from an inferiority complex because of Patrick being the eldest and Bertram being Bertram, so she wonders if you possibly might have another clock to spare and would I mind asking you."

"Why ever didn't she ask me herself before?" said Roberta.

"Oh, you know Clare, she'll have a dozen reasons — afraid you might think her grabbing, afraid that she might be encouraging Becky to grab, afraid lest you haven't really a suitable clock or will rob yourself of one. Have you one, by the way?"

"There's the blue Staffordshire china one with the pink roses; it was to have gone into the sale but of course Becky can have it."

"She'll love that one. I always did," said Naomi.

"But I can't leave Bertram out," said Roberta, "he must have a special present too. I wonder what on earth he would like."

"I could ask now and then I can take it down with the clock tomorrow," said Naomi and disappeared again.

It seemed that Bertram would like the stuffed owl. He could not be found but Patrick firmly vouchsafed for this.

"It's moulting," said Naomi doubtfully, "we put it with the scouts' jumble, but if Patrick says so I expect it's all right."

The clock was a great success after a moment of disappointment as to its relative size.

"But yours is beautiful, Becky, Patrick's is just big," said Naomi, and Becky stroked the clock's overblown china roses lovingly. But when the owl was produced Bertram shouted:

"Take 'im away, take 'im away."

"Oh, dear," said Naomi, "Granny thought that was what he wanted." Patrick looked embarrassed.

"It's norrible Mr Brown," howled Bertram.

"Who?" asked Naomi.

"Stop it, Bertram," said Clare. "What do you mean?"

107

"Mr Brown out of Squirrel Nutkin," explained Becky, "who pulled poor Nutkin's tail off."

"It's *not* Mr Brown, Bertram," said Patrick hastily, "it's Christopher Robin's Owl." But Bertram continued to howl dismally.

"Look here," said Patrick, "I'll have him, Bertram, I'll put him right away from you by my bed with his back to you, so he can't possibly see you — then will you be all right?"

Bertram stopped crying abruptly, as was his wont, and nodded.

Patrick arranged the owl on his little bedside table with much satisfaction. He had always admired him greatly. But that night when they were both in bed Bertram sat up suddenly.

"Patrick," he said, "it's *my* Mr Brown what Granny sent me, Bertram, isn't it, Patrick?"

"Well, yes, I suppose so," said Patrick.

"Goodnight, *my* norrible Mr Brown," said Bertram.

After Naomi had got back from her visits there were only two days left. Roberta was haunted by all the things she had wanted to say and which she now felt would never be said. She longed for the forbidden fruit of emotional satisfaction but she did not dare destroy the delicate comfortable surface relationship between them. She was sure that Naomi would evade any intimate probings with displeasure, though she would not perhaps show resentment so much as slip away and hide behind some trivial topic, shaming her grandmother by turning into a faun or a tree or something equally detached and impersonal. Roberta thought, however, she might venture to ask her whether she intended to come back to Rowanbank again before the move.

"Well," said Naomi, "that depends upon when you go, doesn't it? We shall be going to Vienna to Franz's parents for the Christmas holiday. If you sell before then, I don't think I can come again so soon, unless you need me very badly."

Nothing on earth would have made Roberta press it.

"Oh, I hope to be settled in Coleridge Court by Christmas," she said, "so this is probably your last time at Rowanbank. Do you mind? Will you miss it?"

"Not really," said Naomi. "Well, the view and the garden perhaps, but I have the river and the mountains now instead — Rowanbank is my past." The dismissal was matter-of-fact and serene.

Well, do I want her to be miserable? Why should I mind her not minding? But I do, thought Roberta.

Aloud, and against her better judgement, she heard herself saying: "And I am your past too, I suppose." She meant it to sound like a playful sally, but to her disgust it came out in quite the wrong tone of voice, disgustingly suggestive of hurt. *Now I've done just what I resolved not to do, fish for a response*, she thought despairingly.

But Naomi only answered by one of her rare laughs.

She won't rise, said Roberta to herself, *and it serves me right; but what is to be done with the past then? Surely not simply to discard it like a snake his old skin.*

The following day, the last of Naomi's stay, they piled all the bundles into the hired car to be delivered to their various destinations in the village. At the Oxfam shop they were received by Mr Eliot with gentle courtesy. He was a retired solicitor and presiding over the shop assisted by his big poodle, Gigi, was his refuge from trouble.

"What a gracious day," he said as he took their sacks from them. "Gigi and I are taking our lunch down by the stream, we must catch the last treats of St Martin's summer while we can."

"Oh, dear!" said Roberta when they had left. "Poor man, he's so nice and his wife is so awful. I heard her screaming

109

at him when I passed the house lately. She was drunk, of course; but, drunk or sober, she's a harridan. Yet I believe she was a very handsome woman once. If only she'd die . . . but of course she won't. He always reminds me of a Chekhov character."

"Everyone does, if you think about it," said Naomi.

"Oh, no! Think of Mrs Bun . . . and that reminds me, I must get some bread." Mrs Mugford, the baker's wife, served them. She had a round, brown, fat face and little black eyes like currants.

"Well, I'll grant you Mrs Bun," said Naomi, "but what about Bert Langford? He's straight out of Chekhov."

"Crossed with Dickens, I should say," said Roberta. "His old mother and his curiosity shop are pure Dickens."

"Does his mother still sit in his shop all day?"

"Certainly she does, I'm calling there next to tell him I'm having an auction, though I don't suppose he'll bother about it. He never seems to buy anything fresh and he hates to part with anything. I can't think what they live on."

Bert Langford's shop was at the end of the High Street. In its window was a Chinese vase containing some bulrushes the worse for wear, a huge tabby cat asleep on a carved stool and a small picture painted on glass. The picture was attractive, in soft blues and greens and entitled *The Pensive Shepherdess*; Naomi peered at it.

"I like that," she said, "I might buy it for Franz, he's fond of English antiques."

"But I can let you have something better than that!" exclaimed Roberta. "The whole contents of the big corner cupboard are going into the sale. I'd love you to take your pick. I didn't know you would like something for Franz."

"Oh, thanks, Mother, I'd have said if I'd wanted anything but this is different; I've found this myself. Isn't it rather

110

pretty, don't you think, with the lamb on a ribbon and that dear little church in the background?"

Roberta did not reply. To acquire any fresh object at this moment seemed so unnecessary, even immoral to her; also, in spite of herself, she minded that neither Alex nor Naomi seemed to want or to care for the family things.

They went into the shop. Bert Langford was a frail, bent little man with wispy hair. He wore a very long purple scarf wound round his throat and trailing down his back. In a corner an even frailer and more bent old woman wrapped in a grey shawl sat busily knitting.

"Why, it's Miss Naomi," said Bert, in a surprisingly beautiful low clear voice. "We haven't seen you for a long while."

"How's that cough of yours?" quavered the little old woman.

"I'm very well, thank you, Mrs Langford," said Naomi, "I haven't got a cough."

"Your mother's always so anxious about your chest," said Mrs Langford. "Try two sticks of cinnamon in lots of water morning and night; my mother swore by that and she nursed with Miss Nightingale in the Crimea."

"Thank you very much," said Naomi.

Roberta had begun to turn over a pile of old gramophone records that lay on the counter.

"Oh, Mrs Curling, none of those will do for you," said Bert, shocked, "indeed no."

"I thought I might find one for my grandson," explained Roberta meekly, "but Naomi would like to see the little glass picture in the window."

Bert shook his head sadly. "I'm afraid that's not for sale, Miss Naomi," he said.

"Oh, Bert," said the old woman, "let Miss Naomi have it, now do."

Bert, still shaking his head slowly, removed the pensive

111

shepherdess from the window, dusted her, and at last let Naomi carry her off in triumph.

"Do you think he does it on purpose?" she asked. "To make people want the things more, I mean."

"No, he really loves them and can't bear to part with them. If it wasn't for his mother he'd close down, I believe."

"However old is she?" enquired Naomi.

"No one knows. Now one more call at the scouts' hut and we're done."

On the way home they continued their game of allotting villagers to different authors. Miss Murphy at the Post Office, Roberta decided, was an Agatha Christie.

"She's too sinister for a Christie," said Naomi. "With those pale eyes and her twisted smile, she's more Simenon."

"It's too bad," said Roberta, "she's really a very good daughter to that old paralysed father, but I do admit she is frightening. I'm always giving her the wrong change."

Soon, she thought suddenly, *all these people will become characters in my book of memory.* The vicar was obviously Trollope and they agreed that Mrs Baxter and old Bennet the carpenter were both from Hardy, but they argued over Mr Spires, the schoolmaster.

"You only say he's Lewis Carroll because he looks like the Mad Hatter," said Roberta, "but I assure you he's really Henry James."

They reached Rowanbank in a hilarious mood and Roberta reflected a little sadly, as she got tea, that they met each other more easily and more closely in the world of books than in real life.

The previous morning they had discovered a pile of old piano music in a small tin trunk, gilt-edged volumes of Mendelssohn, Clementi, Chopin.

"Who did these belong to?" Naomi had asked and they had found an inscription in faded ink: "Louisa Mary Willmott — 1860."

112

"I think that must be your great-great-aunt," said Roberta. "I don't remember seeing them before — it's extraordinary what turns up."

Now, this last evening, Naomi brought down one of these albums and started playing. As Roberta sat down to listen, it was immediately borne in upon her that she had heard this particular melody before, long years before and never since, and that it was connected with some unpleasant experience. Then, as it continued, she was no longer at Rowanbank.

It was autumn and she was not even in England. She was a girl again in Bruges, walking the cobbled streets by the side of Sister Marie from the convent school and carrying a basket for her. They came to a tall narrow old house on the Quay de Marbriers, knocked on its door and were let into a lofty, dim room where a white-haired lady wrapped in a black and silver shawl greeted them and was presented with the bottle of home-made wine from the basket.

The lady, who in spite of her hair did not appear old, looked at Roberta so strangely that she felt shy and when Sister Marie rose to go she said, "If you have some other calls to make, dear Sister, perhaps you would leave your pupil here with me for a little while, I do not often have the pleasure of seeing a young girl's face now."

"Of course," said Sister Marie. "You will gladly stay with Madame, will you not, Roberta? I shall not be long."

When they were left alone Madame looked at her again with that curious searching attention and said abruptly, "Do you like music?"

"Yes," answered Roberta.

"Well, I will play for you, but not here. Come with me," and she led the way up great stone stairs until they came to two rooms leading out of each other.

The first room was hung with pale tapestry and seemed

113

full of musical instruments: there was a grand piano, a cello in an open case and what looked to Roberta like a lute decorated with faded ribbons propped against a gilt chair. There was also an easel with a half-finished portrait of a girl upon it. The lady sat down at the piano.

"You will hear me better from my daughter's room," she said, "you are too close to the piano here — go in, please, she will not mind."

Roberta obeyed; there was no question, she felt, of not doing as she was told. The inner room was luxuriously furnished but she had no eyes for anything but a swift impression, for she was riveted by the figure of a girl seated at a second piano, very still and silent. The girl wore a red velvet dress that swept the floor and her black hair was tied back with a red ribbon. She did not move and Roberta faltered on the threshold, wondering what she should do. The light was filtered through the lime trees outside the narrow window and it was only after a long minute or two that she realized that what she was looking at was a life-sized wax figure.

Then the music began. The notes fell softly in slow succession on the air. To Roberta, who had retreated to the window, it seemed as if they turned into the small yellow leaves that drifted down one by one, "brightness falling from the air", to the grey waters of the canal beneath. She stood motionless till the music ceased. Then she tiptoed back into the outer room again.

Madame looked up from the piano. "Did you enjoy it?" she said. "It is my favourite Étude. My daughter plays it also," and Roberta knew somehow that the music in front of the wax figure was the same.

With relief she heard Sister Marie's knock at the front door.

"So she played to you, did she?" said Sister Marie as they went back to the convent. "She must have taken a great

114

fancy to you, poor dear soul. Since her daughter died in an accident she has not been quite as others. She took you to her daughter's room, you say? You are a little upset, I can see. It comforts her, you must understand, that figure. You are Protestant and of course are not used to such dear images — the figures of Saint Cécile and Saint Theresa in my sewing-room, how I would miss them! And the music that Madame played, it is always the same, I believe; it was what her daughter was playing that last morning of her life, you see. Ah, well, she has better music in Heaven, I am sure."

But Roberta had shuddered. The rooms, Madame and the wax figure had been recurring images in troubled dreams for some time afterwards, but she had not thought of them for many ages past.

Now the music had re-created the whole experience for her in startling vividness and she found it still had power to disturb her. Naomi had finished before she had quite recovered the present. "I don't think I have ever heard you play that before," she said. "What is it?"

"One of Chopin's lesser known Études," said Naomi. "No, I don't think I have played it — it isn't Chopin at his best, is it? A bit cloying."

"Yes," agreed Roberta. "Won't you play something else?"

Naomi turned over the pages. "It's not what you'd call a very inspiring collection, but . . . oh, here's some Beethoven."

A serene and timeless little theme washed over Roberta, freeing her from all her tangled emotions. *How foolish to want Naomi to express herself in words*, she thought. *She is a musician and the music says it for her and for me too — it says all I want from her and all she wants, I know, to give me. We know each other perfectly in this.* A deep peace and happiness flowed through her.

Naomi closed the piano and said, "Poor old piano, how I

used to hate you, though of course it wasn't you I really hated, it was music."

"What did you say?" asked Roberta.

"I said I hated music," remarked Naomi lightly, and then seeing her mother's face she added: "Oh, it's all right now, it was only when I had to work at it and worry about it so."

"But I don't understand what you are saying, Naomi," said Roberta, "you couldn't hate music."

"Yes, I did," went on Naomi's clear matter-of-fact voice, "especially the piano — not my flute so much, because that was only secondary."

"But you always wanted to be a musician."

"You wanted it," corrected Naomi.

"But you were so good at it."

"Yes, that was the trouble, I couldn't help that; but I really wanted to be a doctor, a surgeon. I think I would have made a good surgeon." She looked down at her hands.

With a struggle to get out the words Roberta said, "Why didn't you ever say so?"

"Oh, you would have minded so much. Besides, when I was a child I didn't care, and then I took it for granted that you and Father knew best, and later I thought it was my duty because I knew I was good. I went on thinking it was my duty until I met Franz. I can't tell people things or talk about them until they are over. It's really lovely, Mother, not to have to hate music any more."

It was perhaps the most intimate confidential talk Roberta had ever had with her granddaughter and it was an incredible one.

She lay awake that night tossing uneasily trying to come to terms with it. Uppermost was the sense of loss — to have been so mistaken seemed to change the past into a hollow place of false echoes. Then there was self-reproach too to be dealt with. How could she have been so insensitive — was it vicarious ambition that had blinded her? She was afraid it might have been so. She began to talk to Charles as she often did in emergencies. In life he had been her conscience, and the habit of referring everything to him persisted. Sometimes he answered. Reason told her that this was only the natural outcome of their long close relationship, her heart said otherwise.

"Yes, I remember you warned me against pressing the child but I don't believe you guessed what she was really feeling and, oh, the irony of it, Charles! Wanting to be a doctor, I mean. Oh, how strange — and it's not the same Naomi. Oh, Charles, I wish she hadn't told me, I want my Naomi back again."

"Like Madame in Bruges," said Charles.

She lay still for a while after this. "Yes," she admitted painfully, "a wax figure of my own making, dead, in the past. Oh, well, I shall have to be like the snake after all and discard my old skin."

"Not like a snake," said Charles. "Remember Alex's *Wonder Book of Nature* — like a toad, swallow the past and let it nourish the future."

"It's hard," said Roberta, "so hard."

In the morning there was no time for more talk.

Naomi said: "I'll come to Coleridge Court as soon as I can, at Easter perhaps." Her eyes were bright with the anticipation of seeing Franz again. She kissed her grandmother lightly on her forehead and it was if some winged creature had brushed her in passing, then she was gone.

Roberta sat down and wrote a note to the caretaker of the Village Hall, offering the piano and promising to arrange for its removal.

Chapter 10

It was now the end of October; the clocks had gained their hour and the days suddenly seemed closed in and Roberta more than ever before disliked the thought of the long, lonely evening hours. She began to be really anxious about a sale. She had been obliged to find the money for the Coleridge Court flat or she would have lost it, "And heaven knows when another will come your way," Kitty had said. Her bank had been accommodating and had managed a bridging loan, but Roberta was not happy about this and Mrs Baxter was another source of anxiety. Her daughter Betty's baby was due in December and she wanted to be settled in with the family in good time to help.

Viewers were now falling off as the agent had predicted; lately, far from resenting their intrusion, Roberta had welcomed them. She was learning sadly from experience not to build on false hopes. She had had one actual offer only so far. It was from a cheerful weather-beaten lady, only interested in the garden, and that solely in its potential capacity to nourish and amuse two goats, a donkey, four cats and two dogs, all of whom she had rescued from neglect and general misery. Roberta warmed towards her but when her offer proved really too low to be considered, she was relieved that the threat to her father's beloved flowerbeds was removed. Then there was a charming American couple, to whom the Edwardianism of Rowanbank especially appealed. It was apparently quite period enough for them and they enthused over its "art nouveau" alcoves, the fireplaces with their beaten copper hoods and fenders, its leaded windows and gables. They began to plan where to install the extra bathrooms and the radiators for the central heating, but she never heard from them again. There was the large family party who arrived without warning and rushed about as though the place belonged to them already, allotting bedrooms and disputing as to north and south aspects, but though they said they would phone her agent immediately, they too departed for ever.

At last an acceptable offer materialized. It was from an elderly couple, accompanied by a younger, vaguely related pair with whom they were proposing to share the house. All four had looked at the famous view in silence and any comments as they walked from room to room were quietly unfavourable.

"Curious shape this bedroom, isn't it?"

"Does your kitchen face south? That must make it rather hot in summer."

"Mary, mind that awkward little step, this passage is so dark."

Roberta was therefore surprised when the offer came, but she felt she must accept it at once. It was subject to a surveyor's report but this did not worry her unduly, for she believed the house to be structurally sound. She began to hope that after all she might be settled by Christmas.

The surveyor arrived in due course. It was a cold day, and, as he had spent quite a time outside, she invited him in to the sitting-room for a cup of coffee.

"A good period for building, this," he remarked pleasantly. "Not likely to find any dry rot here, that's the worst enemy. Victorian homes are full of it." He made no other comment, but he was a jovial man and his manners confirmed her confidence.

She confided the good news to Mrs Baxter when she arrived the next day with a big bunch of chrysanthemums from the cottage garden — "To cheer things up for you a bit."

"They're lovely," said Roberta, "but I don't want cheering up so much today, Ellen dear. I think I've sold Rowanbank at last — I didn't want to say anything before but I'm almost certain it's going to be all right."

She arranged the flowers in her mother's old blue jug — *though I can't make them look as she did, the witch.* They smelt appropriately of wet autumn leaves, she thought. How stupid of people to grow them in pots all the year round; flowers should keep to their proper seasons. Chrysanthemums actually were not among her favourites but she was grateful for them now; they certainly brightened up the doleful look of the rooms where the removal of various objects showed discoloured places on the walls and thread-bare patches of carpet. A bookseller from Tunbridge Wells, offering her only a little less than Arnold Hathaway's valuation sum, had taken away the books, and the piano had been promptly removed to the Village Hall. Willow was very concerned and stalked around, waving his tail and smelling the emptiness. Roberta congratulated herself that she had not to show any more viewers over a house with such a tatty interior. The board by the gate now said "Under Offer" and she herself now felt "under offer" too, in a sort of no man's land between past and future.

She was by this time down to listing the choice of essentials such as chairs, tables, beds; since these were dictated more by necessity, size, and general utility than by association and sentiment, they were easier to select. But there were many regrets. She would, for instance, have liked to have kept her rocking-chair but it took up too much room; and the pretty round table was discarded in favour of a folding Pembroke one which could be put away when not in use. She was also taking over the dull but still serviceable floor-covering of the flat which she meant to enliven by a couple of her favourite rugs; but Kitty, who was paying her postponed visit, insisted on new curtains.

"It seems an unnecessary extravagance," said Roberta. "I am sure I can cut up some of the old ones to fit — besides, I'm fond of them."

"They're all faded and most of them dreadfully worn. Don't be so stingy and sentimental, Berta. You want something much lighter and brighter to fit those small rooms. Let's send for patterns."

Roberta gave in and compromised by choosing for her new bedroom the old William Morris thrush pattern which had been in her sitting-room, but in yellow instead of red, for the room faced north.

"Are you going to give a farewell party?" asked Kitty.

"What a dreadful idea!" said Roberta. "I don't like parties any more and I hate farewells."

"Well, I don't think you ought just to slink away from Rowanbank," said Kitty. "After all, Uncle built it and you've lived in the village most of your life."

"Who's being sentimental now?" said Roberta. "There's very few left that remember the parents and those few I mean to go and see separately before I leave. But a party. . . . No, I want it all to be over as quickly and quietly as possible, like a death."

"You take it too seriously," said Kitty. "Think how many people are on the move nowadays. All over the world people are moving house; people just don't stay in the same place now, whether they want to or not. I enjoy a move myself; it's a challenge. By the way, I saw a rat yesterday in the attic sitting on that pile of old studio magazines of Charles's that you thought I might like for my hospital."

"Oh, dear!" exclaimed Roberta. "Willow won't go up there any more, in fact he spends more and more time with Mrs B. in the cottage. She keeps a special brand of tinned pilchards that he's partial to. She says he'll settle down much more easily when he has to leave Rowanbank if he gets broken into it gradually by a change of scene now, but rats! I'm glad it was you and not me."

"I said: 'Hullo, Rat, what are you doing here?'" continued Kitty. "He said, 'What are you?' and I said: 'I'm a portent, you'll have to look out for new quarters soon, I can tell you; there'll be changes here, no more nice musty heaps of papers in corners and a younger cat than Willow, I shouldn't wonder, and probably a dog too — a terrier.' He was a sensible rat, if cheeky. He said, 'OK, OK, not to worry — the world's all before me.'"

"I bet he was a young rat," said Roberta. "I take your point, but I'm not you. Unlike yourself, I like to take off my coat and get out my slippers and feel settled. I don't think I'm a natural traveller, at any rate not now, and I devoutly hope I shall never have to move again. And, Kitty, I'm sure I'm not peculiar in hating it all and feeling it traumatic. You know how when you've got an illness everyone cheers you up with horror stories about it; well, Charles's nephew has just had to move because of his job and his wife's had a breakdown and the Mitchells' marriage came to grief because of their move and Alice Rose died when she had to give up her cottage, the one I might have bought."

"Stop it, Berta," cried Kitty. "It's just the reaction from having actually sold the place. Now, do give a party, it'll do you no end of good. Oh, here's Mrs B. — what do *you* feel, Mrs B.? Aren't you glad that you will soon be rid of your cottage and that big garden of yours and starting a new life?"

Oh, Kitty! thought Roberta — but Mrs Baxter only smiled and, to make room for a coffee tray, bore away the jug of chrysanthemums, still glowing though not now at their best.

"I'll bring you a fresh lot tomorrow," she said, "but they'll be the last, I reckon. These are all William's planting; he always did well with his chrysanths. Now Betty's Norman, he's got no use for flowers, grudges them every bit of room he does. Still, there's always window-boxes."

"So there are!" exclaimed Roberta gratefully. It seemed suddenly to her that window-boxes symbolized a humble hope such as surely she could count on for her future. She found them more comforting than Kitty's philosophic rat. Yes, she decided then and there, she would have window-boxes, but she would *not* have a party.

Fate, however, decreed otherwise, for though one can decide not to send out invitations, one cannot prevent them from arriving.

Not long after Kitty had departed, Roberta met the vicar in the Post Office, and he asked her to take tea with him the following afternoon. Charles and she had never been regular churchgoers, in fact Charles, still suffering from his upbringing, had rarely attended except at Christmas and Easter. But Roberta had a deep affection for the church itself and had become fond of the present incumbent. The Reverend Hector Simmons was scholarly, sensitive, conscientious and kind; he was also exceedingly absentminded. This had not mattered greatly while his wife was still alive, for she had kept him in order, but since her death he had become even less reliable. He was self-reproachful and sad about his shortcomings. "I feel I am grieving Marian and letting her down as well as being a nuisance," he confided to one of his long-suffering churchwardens. But his parishioners, who loved him, combined to make good this failing whenever they could and to hide his lapses from him.

The village grapevine functions swiftly, thought Roberta, *he's*

123

probably heard already about the sale and wants to know more about it
and to show me a little extra attention, bless him.

She decided to take him George Herbert's *Country Parson*, which she had discovered among her father's books, as an appropriate parting present. It was a nice little facsimile of an early edition and she hoped he did not already possess a copy.

His eyes lit up as he opened it eagerly, "My dear Mrs Curling, how very kind, but can you spare it?"

Oblivious of her polite assurance and of his housekeeper, Mrs Spence, arriving with an ample tea-tray, he began to read to himself — murmuring at intervals: "What a treasure, what a treasure!" but soon broke out aloud with: "Listen to this now, my dear Mrs Curling: 'When men have nothing to do then they fall to drink, to steal, to whore, to scoff, to revile and all sorts of gamings.' Poor dears, poor dears, how true. Human nature doesn't change much, I fear. Let's see what Herbert advises as a remedy, for it looks as though work for everyone was not the rule even then. 'Husbandry' — well, perhaps, 'the study of mathematics and fortifications' — hmm, hmm, 'the family man has his hands full if he do what he ought to do' — very true, 'for John the Baptist squared out to everyone (even to soldiers) what to do.' Did he now? Indeed, I must look into that, but what's this? 'Love is the Parson's business, wherefore he likes well that his Parish at good times invite one another to their houses and he urgeth them to it and all dine and sup together.' Ha! How very right that I should light upon this in your exceedingly kind gift, Mrs Curling, for it is just the subject I wanted to talk to you about. So if you have had all you want we will draw up our chairs to the fire."

Poor Roberta complied, cast a wistful glance at the untouched tea table and wondered anxiously what was coming.

"I hear you have disposed of Rowanbank," said the vicar, "I hope to your satisfaction. It seems then that you mean to leave us all shortly. It goes without saying that we shall miss you very much."

Roberta, only wishing that it *did* go without saying, murmured that she would miss everyone too.

"Now taking old George Herbert's advice, even before I had read it, I have been thinking that this is one of the times he refers to when we ought to meet together to sup or dine, for there are many I know who would like to say their goodbyes to you and give you their good wishes. So we have planned a little gathering in your honour and I've been asked to invite you and to find out what date and what time would be convenient."

Oh, my, oh, my, thought Roberta, *what a bore and how Kitty will crow, but I must be gracious about it, for it is meant so well.* Aloud she said, "How very kind, but I feel I don't deserve it; it's a long while since I've been much use in the village, I'm afraid."

"Don't you think that perhaps we are never the best judges of how much use we are?" said the vicar. "But talking of use, are those fortunate people who have bought your house likely to be of any? So many newcomers nowadays are with us but not of us."

"I really couldn't say," said Roberta. "Actually they were not very communicative, but that's no guide — I hope at least they will prove a better substitute for my ageing bones."

They went on to discuss other matters. Before Roberta left, however, a date was fixed for the party — the first convenient one, for she felt she would like to get it over as soon as possible. As she was opening the garden gate on her way home, Mrs Spence came running out after her.

"I saw that you didn't get no tea at all, Mrs Curling," she said, "and I'd made a cake on purpose, but as soon as I saw

125

him with his nose in a book I feared how it would be. Now, won't you step round to my room and I'll make a fresh brew? He'll never notice."

Roberta laughed. "It's very kind of you, Mrs Spence, but I want to get home before it's quite dark — it's foggy tonight — though I'm sorry to miss your cake."

She walked back quickly. The village had now almost completely disappeared, she might have been walking on the moon, but even if the mist and the gathering darkness had not obscured the well-known landmarks, Roberta would not have noticed them, she was too busy with thoughts of the party which seemed to bring her departure nearer and confirm its reality. *At least I haven't to worry about whom to invite, which would have been dreadfully difficult*, she thought, *and there won't be room for very many at the Vicarage anyway.*

She found that Mrs Baxter knew all about it already. "I'm to help Mrs Spence with the refreshments — there'll be me and Florrie Mugford and Mrs Spence's niece Doris, and Mercy Brown."

"Surely Mrs Spence doesn't need so many helpers," said Roberta.

"It's well to be properly provided," said Mrs B.

"But the vicar won't be inviting all that number of people," expostulated Roberta.

"There aren't going to be *any* invitations," said Mrs Baxter serenely. "Vicar thought best to let all come who wants and it's not going to be at the Vicarage, it's to be in the Hall."

Oh, the old rascal, thought Roberta. *With his talk about George Herbert's little friendly meetings in each other's homes and all the while plotting to use the Hall, which'll be cold and half-empty and dreadful. Oh, my, as if moving house were not bad enough without all this fuss! Well, I simply shan't think about it any more — "time and the hour runs through the roughest day."*

126

Yet on the day itself, in spite of telling herself that Kitty would say it was she and nobody else who was making the fuss, and though she felt she was behaving exactly like Clare, she was full of nervous apprehension as she set out.

Afraid of being late, she started too early and spent what seemed an uncomfortable time making halting conversation with old Colonel and Mrs Brandon, who were always the first to arrive anywhere. Roberta had turned her back on the door and tried not to look over her shoulder at the trickle of fresh arrivals. The vicar, who was always late, she thought might well forget to come altogether and she was relieved to hear his greeting. After that it was soon all right; the trickle became a steady stream, the Hall began to fill up and to buzz quite loudly and she was able to relax and to welcome the guests. There were many more than she had expected, which was gratifying after all, though she knew that certainly some only came for the outing and the refreshments — old Joe Banks, for instance, whose wheelchair had been pushed within easy reach of the sausage rolls and who, she was sure, was very hazy as to why they had been provided. Not that this mattered in the least; Roberta was relieved to sense that the atmosphere was full of a diffused geniality, not particularly directed towards herself. She felt easily and naturally drawn into its warmth and began to enjoy herself. The heating of the Hall was functioning satisfactorily for a wonder and the place felt comfortable. She thought that Charles's two pictures of the High Street in summer and winter, which she had donated, looked very well, and there was a big pot of autumn berries on Naomi's piano, about which Rachel Lewis, the village organist, was now purring: "Such a generous gift, dear Roberta, and so greatly needed."

By this time Roberta felt she could even do justice to the excellent spread. Mrs Mugford, alias Mrs Bun, the baker's wife, conjured up an easy-chair from somewhere so that she could sit and eat and drink and chat in comfort. *Why really, what angels they all are; you couldn't wish for nicer people*, she said to herself. She knew that such golden thoughts would not persist, but at least she would have had them and this she felt was important. What was it George Herbert had said, "Love is the Parson's business" — well, wasn't it everyone's business?

But now a general lull in the talk occurred and the vicar stepped forward and Roberta realized with horror that he was about to make a speech. She looked away in confusion as he expatiated on her long association with the village, of the sad severance of old ties that would occur when she left them, of the debt of gratitude they owed to her and her family, that their thoughts and good wishes would go with her to her new home and that he hoped she would accept a small token of those good wishes.

He then advanced towards Roberta and handed her an envelope. She opened it and found inside a list of hymns for the next Sunday's service. She glanced up in bewildered amusement but the ever-wary Mrs Spence was at her elbow.

"It was Mrs Baxter who put us up to it, Mrs Curling," she said quickly. "She told us it was no use giving you a book or such like, you were getting rid of so much, but she said you might be going in for window-boxes in London and a garden token for them and some plants to go in them might be acceptable."

"Quite so, quite so," said the vicar, beaming.

"Oh, you shouldn't have," said Roberta, thrusting back the hymn list into the envelope, "it's very very kind of you all. I *do* mean to have window-boxes and what a lovely reminder of you they will be, if I needed reminding, which of course I shan't."

There was a sound of clapping and then Rachel Lewis went to the piano and a group gathered round her. They sang "Jerusalem" and "There is a Tavern in the Town" and "Good King Wenceslas", though it was only November, and ended up inevitably with "Auld Lang Syne". Meanwhile Mrs Spence had slipped away and returned with the token which she had found, as she had expected, on the vicar's desk, and an unperceived exchange was made.

Then Roberta went home. On musing over the evening, she thought how ageless was the sense of a village community and how strong the filaments that bound them together, which she was about to sever. Fearfully and lovingly, she put aside the window-box token and prepared for bed.

Perhaps it was because she was still under the spell of the farewell party that when she opened a totally unexpected letter from her solicitor the next morning her first thought was "a reprieve". For it stated that the surveyor's report on the house had not been favourable after all, that extensive work on the roof and gutters was necessary and in view of this her price must be substantially reduced or the sale was off. Dismay and annoyance, however, soon drove out every other emotion. That traitorous surveyor whom she had refreshed with her best coffee! "That one can smile and smile and be a villain. . . ." Her roof was perfectly sound, she had slept under it in comfort all that year; she didn't believe there was extensive work required. It was an outrage. "They can think again!" she exclaimed as she read the letter through once more, but then she thought of the uncertainty of the future, of being plunged back into that no man's land again and, foolishly perhaps, one of the things that worried her most was the anti-climax it would be to stay on in the village, perhaps for months after that farewell party. Of course she shouldn't have counted her chicken before it was actually hatched. Clare, she remembered, had warned her once, but she had brushed aside the caution as merely Clare's habitual over-anxiousness; now

129

what should she do? Oh, "the slings and arrows of outrageous fortune"!

Kitty, ringing up to know how the party had gone, was for capitulation. "You can't keep Mrs B. away from her daughter much longer and the flat won't improve by being left empty all this time."

"But I can't afford to drop the price so much," wailed Roberta.

"Oh, I expect they'll come round if they really want the place," said Kitty. But, remembering their lack of apparent enthusiasm, Roberta doubted this.

Alex and Naomi were for holding out. "There's as good fish in the sea, or better," said Naomi, and Alex pressed her to come to them when Mrs Baxter had to go.

Roberta was ashamed that the thought of this was so unwelcome. Why, why had she ever consented to move? Well, it was not too late, she could take the house off the market. But Mrs B. was going, the empty spaces in her rooms mocked her, and, if the roof and the gutters were really in such a bad state, they would let the rain and the snow in on her, she supposed, throughout the coming winter. In the watches of the night she could hear Kitty's rat making merry overhead.

Chapter 11

In the midst of this sea of troubles a raft appeared; that same cousin of Clare's, the retired librarian, the once-rejected Morris, wrote out of the blue to say that he found his enforced leisure unsupportable and that he and a sister had decided to join forces and invest their savings in acquiring a suitable property to run as a small guest-house and was Rowanbank still available? Letters and interviews followed and the outcome was that Roberta accepted his offer. She would be slightly better off than if she had reduced her price as demanded, and to sell to Morris would have several advantages. It would please Clare and Alex, it would keep Rowanbank almost in the family, Morris and his sister would, she believed, prove an asset to the village and lastly it gave her some satisfaction to be able to discontinue negotiations with those unenthusiastic conjectural purchasers. Moreover, Morris was willing to adapt his plans to her convenience and this left her free to choose her own time for the move. She found she could accept the idea of Rowanbank as a guest-house without repugnance and could even feel pleasure at the thought of how many people in the future would be able to enjoy her lovely view and her father's garden. She had come a long way since the day when Rose's suggestion that this indeed would be a suitable fate for her home had filled her with horror.

She thought at first that she might, even yet, be in Coleridge Court for Christmas; but Alex and Clare were so insistent that she should spend her first Christmas away from Rowanbank with them that she gave way, and the more readily because both Alex and Kitty would be more free to help her with the move after the festive time was over. So it was settled that as soon as Mrs Baxter left her cottage she should also leave, but that after Christmas she would return for a couple of nights with Kitty for a last pack-up. The removal would then take place, followed by the auction, and then the workmen would move in for repairs and alterations so that Rowanbank Guest-House could open for the summer season.

The weeks now flew by and the morning of Mrs Baxter's departure arrived. Nothing could persuade her from coming round as usual "to see to things".

"Oh, Ellen," cried Roberta, "I'm sure you're too busy at home."

"It's all done, dear; I've only got to go along to the churchyard with a bunch of my Christmas roses. I don't quite know how it is," she explained. "I know William's not there, but it seems something I can still do for him."

"Of course, I understand," said Roberta and she suddenly envied Ellen Baxter. But would Charles have liked her to put flowers on his grave? She doubted it and anyway he didn't have a grave, only a little memorial plate inside the church which was there for her satisfaction not his. "Oh, Ellen," she said after a little pause, "I can't begin to thank you for everything and for being my friend for so long. It's hard to say goodbye."

"Things must change, it stands to reason," said Ellen, "but there's no sense in goodbyes. I'll be thinking often of you, dear Mrs Curling, and you'll sometimes be thinking of me, I dare say."

"Indeed I shall," said Roberta. She watched Ellen Baxter sail majestically down the path, through the gate and across the lane to the cottage for the last time. Then she decided that the best thing she could do straight away was to take the bus into Hastings and buy Christmas presents.

She bought a new paint-box for Becky and a painting-book of her favourite Flopsy Bunnies, in the fond belief that she had inherited her great-grandfather's talent — Becky was still painting her ferocious vermilion houses, Clare wrote, whenever she got the chance. For Bertram, Roberta bought a seductive picture-book containing much useful knowledge about an ant and a bee, and for Patrick, whose latest craze was carpentry, a proper carpenter's measure and a chisel. She believed in useful and edifying presents for children and in frivolous ones for grown-ups; so for Alex she chose a pair of luxurious slippers lined with fur and for Clare, whose shabby grey dressing-gown she had noted with disapproval, she found a glamorous house-coat of tomato-coloured silky material which would set off her dark hair and eyes.

She returned home pleased with her purchases; she had spent a lot of money but felt the better for it and set about the preparations for her visit with improved spirits.

These were dampened on her arrival by finding that she was not to be the only Christmas guest, though she had feared this might be the case, since Alex and Clare were only too prone to indiscriminate hospitality. Jock (she never discovered his other name) was a dour Scotsman, friendless and homeless, Alex explained. On further acquaintance with him, Roberta did not find this too surprising. He smoked, even at meal times, a particularly noisome brand of tobacco, coughed incessantly, occupied the bathroom for an unconscionable period and switched on the television set as frequently and as loudly as possible, so that Roberta felt it a judgement on her for having foisted

133

it on the household. The children, however, had tired of it, she was glad to see.

Patrick and Becky were very busy making Christmas presents and cards and Bertram had invented a new game for himself inspired by the preoccupation of his elders. It was called "Moving House" and involved packing up his toys and books in all the cardboard boxes and plastic bags that he could lay hands on and conveying them from one end of the house to the other. It was difficult not to trip over these, as they were frequently discarded on the stairs or in the passages, but it employed him satisfactorily.

Christmas was observed as a strictly demythologized festival in Clare and Alex's household.

"I'm sure you understand, Gran," said Alex, "we can't tell the children what we don't believe ourselves."

And Roberta, thinking of her mother, felt: *Who am I that I should not understand?* Yet, as in the case of television, she believed that Alex and Clare did not allow enough for outside influences. Patrick and Becky seemed to her to be very muddled and she considered all three children deprived.

They had not been allowed even the brief midnight magic of Father Christmas, let alone the shepherds, the Wise Men and the star. Becky had once asked: "Why does Father fill our stockings instead of Father Christmas — is it because we are bad? He comes to *all* my friends." *Well, Father Christmas must take his chance*, thought Roberta. *After all, he is only an inhabitant of Looking-Glass Land; but for the rest I'll go surety.* And partly from worthy motives and partly, it must be confessed, from unworthy — for her dear Alex and Clare always seemed to arouse in her a spirit of opposition — she decided to take the children to see the Crib in St John's Church down the road. This was a huge, grim Victorian building usually kept closed for fear of vandalism but because it was Christmas week it was open for several hours each day with a custodian on duty. Becky and Bertram, who had never been inside any church before, were at first abashed by its sheer monstrosity and Patrick was in a mood of benevolent interest, so no one spoke till they got to the side chapel, where there was a large well-peopled stable.

The children stood in a row and stared, then Patrick said, "That sheep's much too big, I think . . . why, he's almost as big as the ass, and the ass oughtn't to be the same size as the ox. I wish I had my measure here to measure them."

"Hush," said Roberta, casting a look behind her. "Don't speak so loudly." But her own voice was drowned by Bertram's shrill one.

"Are they going to eat the baby?" he enquired eagerly.

"No, of course not," said Roberta, hoping against hope that the custodian was out of earshot.

"When I grow up," said Becky dreamily, "I'm going to have two dear little babies, one called Flopsy and the other called Jesus."

"You can't call them that, silly," said Patrick, "Flopsy is a rabbit's name — you're always mixing up animals with people — and nobody's ever called Jesus."

"But animals *are* people," said Becky, "and Jock's got a dog called Bobby, and why doesn't people call their babies Jesus? He was a very nice man."

"He wasn't exactly a man, that's why," said Patrick. "Do explain, Gran."

Roberta hesitated. She thought she heard laughter in Heaven, explain the eternal divine paradox! Should she give them a dusty answer? — "You'll understand when you're older." But she did not really believe that understanding was required or even possible. She put up a swift prayer, which to her astonishment was answered no less swiftly.

Suddenly and magically the organ burst forth above.

Unperceived, someone had come to practise for the carol service. As the great notes of "Adeste fideles" rolled gloriously out over their heads, the children were startled into silence and also, at last, into something like awe. The sound ceased as abruptly as it had started while the organist found his next score and Roberta hurried her flock away. Becky and Bertram ran noisily down the aisle but Patrick came slowly. He did not resume his questioning and Roberta thought that the music was a better answer than any she could have provided.

She did not expect to enjoy her Christmas Day very much, and nor did she. In the first place, she was really a little sated with Christmases which, as she grew older, seemed to recur more and more frequently, another coming up before the chimes of last year's carols had died on the air. Then she had to fight the nostalgia for Rowanbank and the past that threatened, unless she were careful, to engulf her. With the children around she could not count on much peace but at least they brought with them the compensation of their own excited happiness. The same could not be said of Jock, whose addiction to tobacco and television was telling progressively on her nerves: but a mild complaint was met by Alex with the shocked response: "Poor fellow, he has so few pleasures."

There is, however, such a powerful compulsion on Christmas Day itself to please or to be pleased, that the hours generally pass benignly. So Roberta managed to sustain with commendable grace the dawn chorus of children, the fraught ceremony of giving and receiving gifts, cousin Morris and his sister to dinner and an interminable evening's entertainment provided by Patrick and his friend Martin.

She took herself off to church in the morning, though not to St John's (where she feared to meet the eye of that custodian), and hurried back after the service, so as not to keep the family waiting for the present-giving ceremony. Everyone seemed pleased with what she had chosen for them and she herself was touched by Patrick's gift, over which he had obviously taken much trouble. It was a large collage neatly framed in plywood, depicting a bright blue sea with white crinkly paper waves into which a huge scarlet sun was setting, while a ship with a fine sail was entering the brown tweed harbour walls. Underneath was written in bold, though somewhat unequal letters: "SAFE HOME."

"It's an alligator," said Becky. "Patrick, let me do the sun — isn't it beautiful!"

"She means an allegory," said Patrick hastily, "about your moving, Gran. I did most of it at school in art and Miss Brown helped me a little but I did the frame at home all by myself. Do you like it?"

"It's splendid," said Roberta, wondering what on earth she should do with it. She decided it must live under her bed, to be brought out and given a place of honour whenever the children came to Coleridge Court. For the time being, she bore it away to her bedroom and propped it up against her looking-glass. She trusted it was a good augur for the future — *I only hope I shall feel "safe home" again one day*, she said to herself and lay down for a little rest before dinner.

Clare was busy in the kitchen. She had refused help — "It only confuses me, thank you all the same," she had said to Roberta — and was having to concentrate resolutely on what she was doing, as her mind was perturbed on three counts. First her guests, unfortunately not being vegetarians, might sadly miss their turkey, bacon and sausages.

"Oughtn't we to provide them with the horrid stuff?" she had said to Alex, but he had answered:

"Not on our lives."

So, secondly she was anxious that the substitutes should

137

do justice to the family's principles and, indeed, was not without hope that they would prove delicious enough to convert at least Morris and his sister. She had no hope of Roberta. Lastly she was praying that everyone would get on with everyone else, that Bertram would behave nicely, that Jock might, with luck, not show up at all and that Morris would not talk too much about Rowanbank, which might upset Granny. This, however, she need not have feared.

Roberta, though she still found him tedious and ceased to listen when he held forth on all the possible and impossible heating systems in vogue, was touched by his enthusiasm and also, as she looked down at the undistinguished cutlery and thought how her lost silver would have embellished the table, she was overcome with self-reproach that she had rejected him in favour of that specious rogue Hathaway. Laura, Morris's sister, was a small, bright bird-like woman with a habit of clicking her false teeth at the end of each speech, which added a peculiar emphasis to her otherwise mild remarks. She was in her mid-fifties and had lately been released by death from a life of subjection to a fierce invalid mother from whom, of course, Morris — though the adored one — had early freed himself. No one had thought this unfair or strange. Roberta hoped that Laura was not now exchanging one thraldom for another, but she decided this was unlikely unless it had become a habit, for Morris was a gentle man and also used to looking after himself. They were both full of eager plans and had already two prospective long-term guests in view.

"We mean to attend your auction (click click)," said Laura, "for even between us we find we haven't enough furniture for all your lovely great rooms. Mother and I only had a small flat at Putney, you know. You wouldn't object to us buying in some of your things (click click)?"

"Of course not," said Roberta, "I'd like to think of them being still there."

"That's what I told Laura," said Alex. "The sideboard, for instance, you'll need a good sideboard for a guest-house and it would be a pity to move that one, it fits in the recess so well."

"We may not get it," said Morris, "in fact you ought to be hoping it will catch the dealer's eye, but you don't know much about such things, I believe, Alex. It all depends on the demand, of course; large furniture isn't so much sought-after these days. Now our grandfather, Clare, if you remember, was quite an authority on period pieces — he told me that you must always look at the back and the inside of drawers. I'll tell you why."

Oh, thought Roberta, *he's off again*; but she felt that for both Morris and Laura moving house was romantic, an alluring adventure, an expansion of their lives, and this was in every way a complete contrast to what she herself was experiencing.

Clare brought in the Christmas pudding in triumph. She was feeling relaxed at last — everything had turned out well after all, the children's behaviour had been exemplary and Jock was mercifully still sleeping off his Christmas Eve revels in the boys' bedroom.

The evening was devoted to Patrick's ENTERTAINMENT. Becky and Bertram could not remember a Christmas without this event but in reality of course it was only since the six-year-old Patrick, after having been taken to his first pantomime, invited the family to an ENTERTAINMENT, consisting of a rapid recitation of nursery rhymes given in varied and elaborate costume which involved long intervals between each item. This had been repeated each year with steadily increasing ambition, until now it included Becky and Bertram and his best friend Martin, and had taken on the semblance of a play. It retained, however, the same characteristic lengthy preparations and intervals with the briefest of scenes and dialogue.

On the whole the elders welcomed the ENTERTAINMENT as employing the children happily while they were left in peace, all that was asked of them being free access to the "dressing-up" chest and enthusiastic applause. *Are there any creatures who at the same time manage to be so boring and so interesting as children?* Roberta wondered to herself as she gazed at Patrick who, with an army cap that had once belonged to George falling over one eye, waved a cardboard sword over Martin, wrapped in Bertram's scarlet bed quilt, lying slain at his feet. Becky, in an old white lace curtain, cheered from a tower of perilously piled stools. It was clear that a romantic rescue was in process, but it was difficult to know who Bertram was or what he was supposed to be doing. He wore a green paper crown from one of the morning's crackers and a spangled evening cape long ago discarded by Clare and sat silently and apart under a red umbrella. Perhaps he was a fairy.

Roberta, gazing, considered her great-grandchildren anew. In their grotesque garb they presented a fresh aspect, and she caught now and then a hitherto unsuspected family resemblance flitting momentarily across their faces. This fascinated her. They looked flushed and serious. The distillation of absurdity and charm in their performance held her spellbound and she felt a sudden wave of protective tenderness towards them. If only she possessed an enchanter's wand she would have waved it to keep them as they now were, safe in the present. So soon "the painted birds would cease to laugh in the shade", so soon the play would be over and Patrick's ENTERTAINMENT no longer be one of the wonders of the world. But she shook off the thought at once. As if that would keep them safe! What a mockery all this silly sweetness would be if they were never to grow out of it, to be "on the move" from innocence to experience.

There was a sound of clapping round about her. The actors were leaping across the room — "Did you like it? Did you like it?" they cried. "It was much the best yet, wasn't it?"

Boxing Day is not generally one of the easiest in the year's calendar. Perhaps it was better when there were twelve days of Christmas; as it is, it must always be something of an anti-climax and, besides, has to contend with hangovers, indigestion and the reaction from the extra good behaviour of the previous day. Clare was thinking gloomily along these lines as she opened the sitting-room window as wide as it would go, to let in air after Jock's nightly occupation. *Granny will hate it smelling like this.* It really was rather a nuisance having him with Gran in the spare room and she wished he would at least fold up his blankets. She hoped Alex would take him off for a walk soon and she would send the children out and that should secure a little peace. Just then Roberta, who meant to spend the morning writing to Naomi, came into the room. She had not slept well and felt low and as she opened the door a chill north-easterly blast met her.

"Gracious, Clare, it's December, must we have the window open so wide or even at all?"

"I thought you hated the smell of smoke," said Clare, "that's why I opened it."

"Well, yes, I do," said Roberta. "It's a choice between two evils then, I suppose, but it really does feel very chilly in here."

"I'll leave it open just a crack, shall I, and turn up the heating?" said Clare, soothingly.

But Roberta, sensing the soothing and resenting it, said, "It will take some time for that to be effective. It seems to me that radiators are always too hot or not hot enough; you never get the comfortable warmth that the old fire

141

gave. I hate the idea that I shall only have radiators in the flat. It is a pity, I think, that you and Alex didn't keep just one open grate."

I know you think it, said Clare to herself, *and have said so several times, dear Granny, but surely we can do what we like with our own house.* Her patience, which that morning was not of first-class quality, was wearing a bit thin and she had to remind herself that old people were usually touchy about temperatures. "I'm just going to turn out the children to get some fresh air," she announced brightly.

"I should have thought they would get enough of it in here," said Roberta and immediately commented silently: *I shouldn't have said that, I really am rather a nasty person I'm afraid.*

But Clare only said, "I'm afraid it may rain later. I hope Alex has taken his raincoat."

Yes, that's what annoys me about Clare, thought Roberta, *that's what I find depressing: she's the sort of person who always thinks it's going to rain.* She sat down to her writing, hoping that in describing Patrick's play and Laura Morris's curious clickings to Naomi she would recover cheerfulness and good behaviour.

Clare, by means of bribes and threats, persuaded the children to get on their outdoor things and go into the garden. She then returned to the sitting-room with some sewing. *I'm really very fond of Gran,* she told herself firmly, *but being fond of a person doesn't always seem to be enough. Perhaps I didn't thank her properly for that lovely present. . . . I wish I knew what to do with it. I'm not the sort of person that wears housecoats, and my dressing-gown is still quite good and much warmer. I wonder if I could make it into a dress; I need a new dress so badly and it's a lovely material, though a bit bright. Yes, I shall try and do that.* The thought pleased her and she set herself to think of something to say, for the silence had lasted too long and her grandmother was folding up her letter.

Roberta, too, felt that there should now be some

comfortable conversation. *Clare and I have the best intentions,* she thought a little sadly, *but we don't mix chemically very well. I don't suppose it matters much, however, for we are both nice people, or at least fairly nice.*

The children's voices in the garden were clearly to be heard in the quiet room through the slightly open window and suddenly these became louder and disputatious.

"I'm going in now," Patrick was saying, "I've got work to do."

"No, no!" shouted Becky and Bertram. "We can't play Old Man without you."

"You must play something else then."

"Shan't," roared Bertram.

"Hi, Bertram, where are you going?" cried Patrick.

"To fetch Gran."

"Gran can't play Old Man; she's too old, she can't run."

The garden door slammed and then Bertram shouted: "Stupid Old, stupid Old!" and burst out crying.

Clare jumped up. "Oh, how naughty!" she exclaimed. "Really, Bertram! I'm so sorry, Granny."

"Don't fuss, dear," said Roberta, "Bertram's absolutely right, 'stupid old' it is. I wish more people saw it like that. *I'm* as eager and willing to play and run as ever — I don't mind about draughts and fires, I can jump over the moon —it's just 'stupid old'."

But Clare was not listening, for she had already left the room.

Roberta, however, continued the conversation with herself: *That's what I must always remember, I must never let "stupid old" become me.* With this blessed sense of detachment the burden of the day seemed lifted. She became charitable and, till lunchtime, entertained a pacified Bertram with a fourfold reading and rereading of the Ant and the Bee.

Clare, thankful to leave them together, retired to her kitchen, deciding to avoid thinking about either of them for the present. Feeding her family and her guests over the holiday had its problems, but they were not complicated like some.

The next day, Kitty arrived to convey Roberta back to Rowanbank. She had been busy with Christmas at her hospital, but was as usual cheerful, energetic and tactless, either by nature or design, Roberta could never quite make up her mind which.

"You look washed out, Clare. I always say give me an institutional Christmas rather than a family one. Roberta, I hope you at least are in good shape — you'll need to be."

"Why do you say such things?" she demanded as they started on the homeward journey.

"What things?" asked Kitty.

"Well, for instance why depress me by the awful shape of things to come?"

"You looked too happy to leave poor Clare," said Kitty. "You and Alex never notice how she slaves."

"She was born a slave," said Roberta with guilty emphasis, "and no one could possibly call Alex selfish."

"He doesn't remember that charity begins at home," said Kitty.

"You're not fair, Kitty, it's just that he thinks of Clare as part of himself."

"Exactly," said Kitty. "But I didn't mean to depress you about the move. It will be fun."

Roberta reflected. Yes, it was true she was happy to exchange Clare for Kitty, for with Kitty it did not matter whether it rained or no.

She found her bracing companionship invaluable over the following week, for it proved a traumatic time. Each morning she woke in a panic which resolved into a pattern of apprehension: how was she ever to be ready in time? What had she to do that day? What vital detail had been forgotten? But by breakfast this whirlpool had subsided and was succeeded by the merciful sense of unreality which had, at intervals, taken over ever since she had first decided on the move.

She spent the days busily on packing, finishing off her new curtains, giving and receiving last goodbyes and making and losing and remaking her beloved lists. Kitty bought three sets of coloured tickets, red for the articles to be removed to Coleridge Court, blue for the goods to be auctioned and green for the few pieces to be sent to Alex and herself. It was while she was fixing on the red labels to one after the other of the objects she had chosen to take with her that the thought occurred to her: *These are all bits of my past — childhood, my parents, friendship, lovers, marriage, children. Why, I've been moving house all my life.* She sat for some time musing on this and it seemed to her a momentous enough idea to share with Kitty.

"Very fine and metaphysical," said Kitty, "but now please confirm the time the removal van will be here and phone Coleridge Court about the keys, and don't forget you promised to see if that young couple in Mrs B.'s cottage will be of any help to Laura and Morris."

Ellen and William Baxter's successors had moved in just before Christmas and Roberta had hardly seen them yet. Now she braced herself to call and it needed some courage, for she was missing Ellen at every turn. A large smart car blocked the cottage path and she had to step on to the flowerbed to round it. On the further side a young man was busy cutting down the old pear tree. True, it was long past good fruiting and obscured the light, but — "Change, change in all around I see," Roberta muttered as she rang the door bell. A fair, top-heavy girl in tight jeans and an enormously wide thick pullover answered it.

"Mrs Forbes?" enquired Roberta. "I'm Mrs Curling from Rowanbank."

"But she didn't use surnames, of course," said Roberta to Kitty afterwards. "They're Samantha and Don and I was Roberta in no time and Ellen's kitchen is bright red and the stairway's got stars painted all over it."

"Well, I think that's rather nice," said Kitty. "And as for names, away with barriers I say. You couldn't expect a young William and Ellen, but I bet you did, and a couple of their babies playing in the garden, but the point is are they going to be of any use?"

"Not much, I'm afraid, she's got a job in a shop in Rye, but she said she'd do what she could at weekends. She's friendly enough, seemed pleased that Rowanbank is going to be a guest-house. 'Bring some life to the place,' she said."

"Then that's another thing off our minds," said Kitty. "Don't look so glum."

Roberta laughed. "I suppose everything being so different ought to make it easier to leave. Nothing can stay the same, I know, but why then does one mind so much that it changes?"

Chapter 12

On the day before the move was to take place, Roberta had slept late, tired out by all the endless unforeseen details that had to be attended to. She woke to a strange white light and an unearthly stillness and, suspecting what she would see, she threw a shawl over her shoulders and went to the window. A charm of snow lay over the countryside — it was the first fall of the winter and, as always, seemed to Roberta momentous and fantastic. The familiar landmarks were transformed or altogether blotted out, the low round hills melted into the sky, paths had disappeared, hedges bowed low, distinctions of tone and colour were non-existent. This withdrawal into anonymity of her beloved view seemed to Roberta like a gesture of farewell.

She sighed and hastened into the warmth of the sitting-room. Telephone bells began to ring.

"At least we are not cut off," said Kitty.

"Clare always said this would happen if I moved in January. I do wish she wasn't so often right," said Roberta. "Will everything have to be put off?"

But it appeared that, if there were no further falls and no disastrous thaw followed by a freeze, all would go ahead as planned: Alex would arrive at nine o'clock the next day to take Roberta to Coleridge Court, leaving Kitty to follow with the men and van.

"Are you sure you'll be able to manage, Kit?"

"Of course. I'm an old hand. They're certain to be nice men, you'll see."

"Alex has taken the day off," said Roberta. "He's going to help me get straight."

"Good, you'll need to feel at home as soon as possible in this weather. And won't you be glad of the central heating, you old Spartan?" said Kitty.

No further snow fell and Roberta did not know whether she was glad or sorry. The hours of waiting now seemed endless, as waiting so often does, yet she clung to them; as long as they lasted, she was still herself — still at home. During the brief daylight the sun failed to pierce the gunmetal sky and any light there was seemed to come from the snow-laden earth.

Kitty cleared a space in the garden upon which to scatter crumbs for the birds. "It isn't deep," she said, "it ought to be all right." Later Roberta caught her coming down from the attic. She looked guilty and was carrying an empty saucer.

"Kitty," Roberta exclaimed, "don't tell me you've been putting food out for that rat?"

"Well, I expect he's terribly hungry," said Kitty, "it'll keep him from foraging below stairs. You were too fast asleep but I heard him last night. Besides, don't you want him to have lovely last memories of Rowanbank? He'll be off as soon as the builders move in."

"Oh, Kit!" cried Roberta and suddenly wanted to laugh and cry at once.

The next day, though the snow remained, the roads had been cleared and the removal men arrived punctually, but when Roberta opened the door for them she was dismayed to see two frail-looking little gnomes grinning up at her. Even Kitty was taken aback and rushed to the kitchen to put on the kettle, muttering: "Best fatten them up a little before anything else."

The gnomes, however, seemed both friendly and capable and, after consuming mugs of strong sweet tea, set about their work without delay. The smaller of the two seemed to be in charge. He assumed at once a fatherly attitude towards Roberta.

"Now don't you worry, lady," he said, "the weather's OK, there won't be much on the roads this morning, and so we'll get along all the quicker, but we can't have you catching cold. You leave everything to me and my brother, we've never hurt or harmed a piece yet, have we, Ned?"

Ned nodded and patted the frame of the mirror. "Nice bit here," he said appreciatively.

"You do understand, only the things with the red and green labels are to go to London — the blue ones are to stay here."

"Yes, lady," said the chief gnome. "Pity, though, I don't like homes broken up, see? Fanciful, I know, but seems as though all these pieces have got used to living together."

I never expected removal men to be so human, thought Roberta. *Perhaps it's because they're such small ones — I do hope they'll be equal to lifting and carrying everything. It's a good thing they haven't got to cope with the piano.*

Actually, however, once they set to they began to deal with the furniture so rapidly that she was relieved when Alex's car arrived for it was certainly time to be off if she was to arrive at the flat before the van, so she drove away at last in a bustle and had no time to think or to feel.

There was no snow at all in the London streets, only in the garden of Coleridge Court little patches of irrelevant whiteness showed up under the bedraggled bushes. It all appeared rather sordid and desolate. "Get a kettle on as soon as you arrive," Kitty had said, "tea's the priority in a move," and she had packed a basket with the necessities and thrust it at Roberta on parting so that, obediently obeying instructions, she did not stop to consider anything but that the flat seemed warm, that the gas cooker was functioning and that the rooms looked too small for anything but dolls' furniture. This dismayed her, but almost at once the van drew up before the door and Kitty marched in.

"Here we are again," she announced loudly. "Have you got tea ready? My dear, they're twins, Fred and Ned, absolute pets."

The gnomes, who had followed close behind, looked gratified and accepted their ritual mugs with pleasure and soon all once more was in rapid motion.

"Let's get lady's bed in first and make it nice and comfortable for her," said the fatherly Fred.

Does he expect me to jump into it here and now? thought Roberta. *I only wish I could.* Instead she found herself breathlessly busy. Ejected from the van with remarkable rapidity, each object demanded an immediate resting place. The larger pieces presented no difficulty; it was the little articles and worst of all those unwanted, forgotten shamemaking bits and pieces — a shabby wastepaper basket unaccountably still full of rubbish, old boxes with forgotten rusty tools, an incredible pair of Charles's wellingtons — where had they been hiding and what on earth should she do with them? Fred and Ned carried each bit of rubbish tenderly in and set it down carefully in the tiny hall. *Surely that must be all now, thank Heavens*, thought Roberta, for there was a lull at last. But it was *not* all. She looked out of the window and saw, blocking up the whole approach, the large old garden seat. It looked enormous out of its context.

The gnomes, having lowered it on its side, edged round it and called to her, "Where shall we take this, lady?"

"But it ought never to have come!" exclaimed Roberta.

"I told him," suddenly spoke up the hitherto subservient

Ned, "it didn't have no red label. I told him but he don't listen to me."

· "Easy now, Ned," said the other, "it didn't have no blue one neither. It was like this, lady, see, this here was lying on it and this had a red one on, OK, so I took it that both was meant to come together."

He held out a small bundle of gardening tools, a little weeding fork and trowel and a pair of secateurs and a pair of gloves, all of which Roberta had put together with her window-boxes in mind. She remembered now having left them on the bench after labelling them and she supposed she had overlooked the bench itself — perhaps the snow was to blame, but it was no use bothering about that now.

"Yes, I quite understand," she said to Fred, "but I can't think what we can do with it."

"Oh, well," said Alex, "something like this was bound to happen. It'll just have to go back again, that's all."

Fred scratched his head. "That'll be arkard," he said, "we got another move on today before we finish, down Essex way; just time for it, and we'll want all the room in the van we can get."

They all stood and looked at the seat, which lay there obstinately asserting its right to exist.

"Wait a sec," said Kitty suddenly, "I've got an idea. Your phone's connected, isn't it, Roberta?" She vanished but reappeared again very soon.

"It's all right, I got on to the warden at once and she says to put it in the square garden for the time being, and your garden key is hanging behind the kitchen door — oh, and she says she hopes everything is all right and will you let her know if you want anything."

The gnomes' faces cleared and they carried the seat across the road. It was set down under a big old lilac tree where it at once took on an air of permanence. "Pity it can't stay there; it looks at home, like," said Fred.

151

"Well, who knows," said Alex, "it might be possible. I should think the tenants would welcome it and it would make it seem more like your garden, wouldn't it, Gran?"

Roberta assented vaguely; she did not at the moment feel that the square could ever seem like her own garden, but she was too tired to care. She was conscious only of relief that a crisis had been at least temporarily resolved and that soon the men would go and she could relax. This, after a final round of tea, they proceeded to do, taking Kitty with them.

"Fred says he'll drop me at the Angel," Kitty said. "I've got to be at the hospital by four today, but I'll come round as soon as I can tomorrow to help get you straight."

"I can't be grateful enough to you," said Roberta. How kind everybody was being, she thought, and what a nuisance she was. Now here was Alex starting already to hang her curtains and pictures.

"I'll just get these out of the way and then perhaps we could have something to eat," he said. "Tea's all very well but I'm starving."

"I've got enough food here somewhere," said Roberta, "only I don't know where anything is."

"We'll go out then," said Alex. "Is this where you want the mirror? There! That's a good job done!"

But Roberta, who had carefully planned her walls beforehand, now saw that the total effect was wrong.

"Oh, Alex!" she exclaimed. "The *Still Life* — I thought it would fit nicely there, but it's crowded by the door, and the landscapes are too high, and the mirror too low — oh, why am I such a fool?"

She was in a daze of exhaustion, exasperation and grief.

"Come and eat," said Alex.

When they got back she certainly felt better but the pictures still looked wrong.

"The Japanese say about their gardens: 'If you place

152

stones in the wrong order your house will fall down.' So it is important," she pleaded.

"Well, I'll alter them then," said Alex cheerfully; "not to worry, but then I must be going."

"I've kept you too long already," said Roberta. "Clare will think there's been an accident."

She sat back and watched and saw that she had been right and wondered why the correct placing of objects mattered so much. It was of immense comfort, she felt that it should be so, a sort of reassurance about the universe.

"There's more snow forecast," said Alex, drawing the newly hung curtains, "we've been lucky it's held off today. If we're in for a bad spell now it'll be such a comfort to know that you're snug and warm here instead of shivering away at Rowanbank."

"I'll fetch your coat, dear," said Roberta without comment.

After he had gone, she sat motionless before the place where the fire ought to have been and stared round at the strange little box in which, unaccountably now it seemed, she found herself. She sought some assurance of continued identity from the few household goods she had brought with her but, removed from the surroundings she had always known them in, they appeared unfamiliar, as if she were seeing them for the first time. She realized that it was long since she had actually looked at them at all — that queer little cupboard, for instance, that really handsome mirror, that rug, nice but worn. . . . Her eyes travelled over them critically as objects existing in their own right, unencrusted by associations. She herself felt curiously weightless and empty and a little dizzy. "Lawks a mercy, this is none of I," she quoted fearfully to herself.

Presently she made an effort to find the necessary equipment for a meal, which was a difficult and lengthy process. Then she went to bed. She was tired out but she could not sleep. It was neither dark nor light, for a lamp outside could not be satisfactorily excluded; neither was it noisy or quiet, since through the window, open because of the heating, came the unremitting roar of London which sounded even more clearly as, hour after slow hour, the nearer noises were hushed. Every now and again the radiator gave a gurgle and Roberta listened for it and hated it. The sense of lost identity grew stronger and she began to panic.

"I've made a mistake, I've made a great mistake," she said aloud, "I must go back." But she knew she couldn't.

At last she fell into an uneasy doze in which she was searching feverishly for something, she did not know what, that was gone beyond recall. She was wakened by the ringing of her telephone and stumbled out of bed to answer it.

"Roberta Curling speaking," she said, and hoped this still was true. There was no reply but she distinctly heard a sound of deep breathing. "Who is it?" she enquired anxiously.

Silence — then a high shrill voice proclaimed: "It's me, Bertram, me!"

"Oh," said Roberta with relief. "Oh, darling, how lovely to hear you! How are you? How clever of you to phone."

No reply, only another long pause and then rather faint and far away: "Goodbye . . . goodbye."

But Roberta did not ring off, for she could still make out the breathing and at last, just as she was giving up, there came a loud triumphant "Hullo" and then the receiver clicked back into place.